# Take a Chance

## Sawyer's Cove: The Reboot

**Libby Waterford**

# Also by Libby Waterford

**Sawyer's Cove: The Reboot**

Take Two

Take a Bow

Take it All

Take a Chance

Take Me Over

Hot Take in Steamy Shorts: A Kissed by Romance Anthology

Take Another Look in A Kiss at Midnight: A Kissed by Romance Collaboration

**Never a Bride**

Can't Help Falling in Love

Can't Make You Love Me

Can't Fight This Feeling

Can't Hurry Love

**Weston Reunion**

Flirting with Her Professor

Her Reunion Fling

Falling for Her Ex

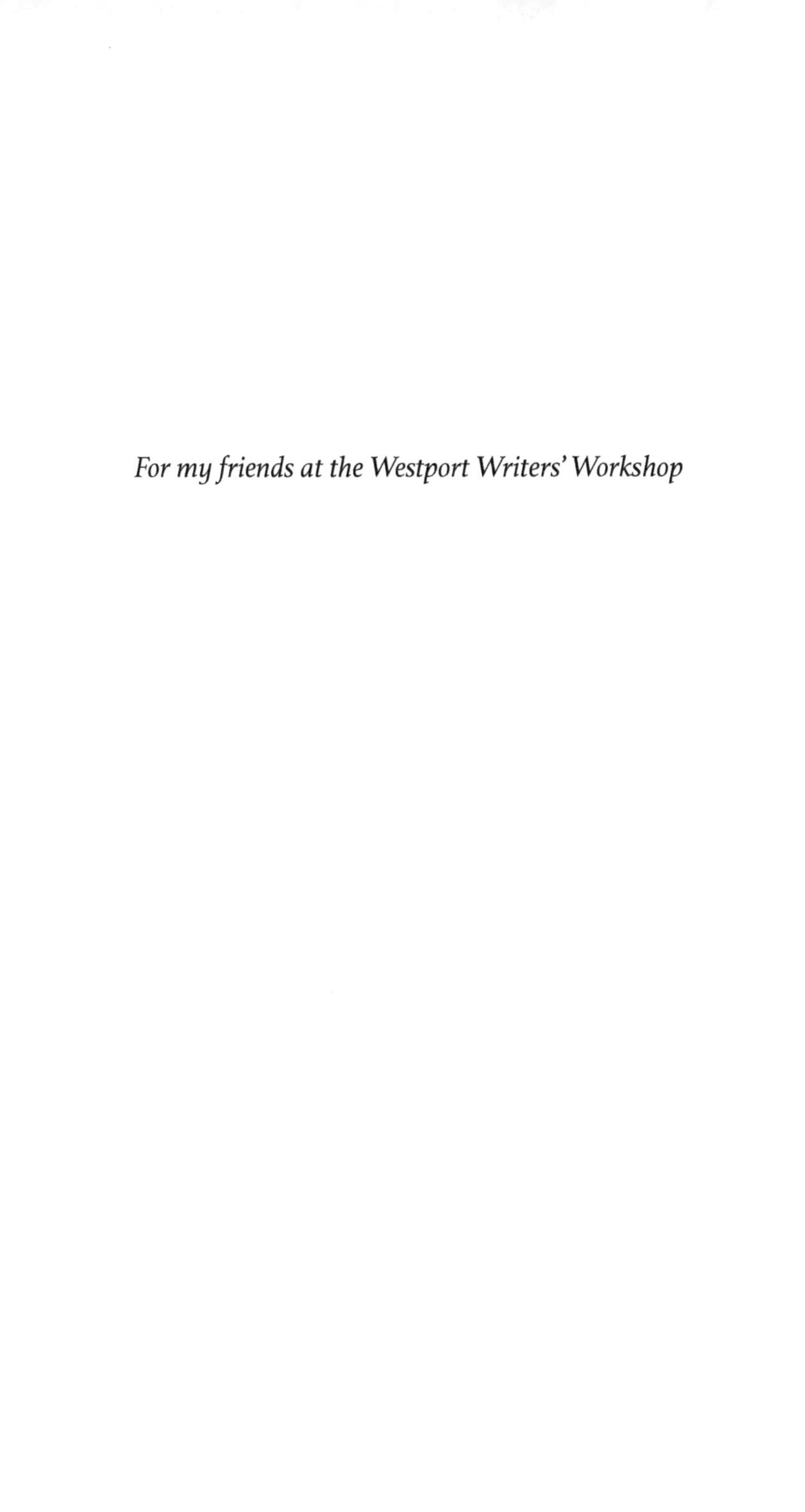

*For my friends at the Westport Writers' Workshop*

"If you obey all of the rules, you miss all of the fun."

— Katharine Hepburn

# Chapter One



*December 25*$^{th}$

"Let's play a game," Darren Silverstein said. Desperation dripped from his voice.

Crosby could relate. The last ninety minutes had been excruciating. He'd accepted Darren's offer to share his Misty Harbor Inn room for the night because he'd had no choice—a winter storm had arrived in the small Connecticut seaside town early, and it hadn't been safe to drive his sports car back to New York on the interstate.

To make matters worse, there was no room at the inn, or anywhere else in Misty Harbor on Christmas Day. Luckily for Crosby's physical well-being, Darren had an extra bed.

Unluckily, the forced togetherness had been about as awkward as Crosby had feared.

They'd made it through the delivery of their room service dinner with the minimum of conversation—which meant the minimum of antagonism. But after the food had been consumed and trays relegated to the hallway, they'd both started fidgeting.

It was too early to go to sleep. Neither of them had swimsuits, so the indoor pool was out. It was Christmas Day, two hours into what was forecast to be a significant winter storm. Crosby didn't want to make more work for the people who worked at the inn by wandering around, looking for something to do.

Crosby could have gotten out the script he was studying for an upcoming audition, but he was oddly reluctant. What if Darren asked questions about the part? He could have thrown his earbuds in and listened to the podcasts he'd planned to catch up on during his drive home from Misty Harbor before the weather changed his plans, but he doubted he'd be able to concentrate on anything with Darren sitting six feet away.

"I like games," Crosby said cautiously. "We could play the movie game."

"Or 'Truth or Dare,'" Darren responded, as if he hadn't heard Crosby's suggestion.

"Are we twelve?" Games appealed to Crosby's competitive side, and he was usually the first to volunteer to play. But he could imagine too many disastrous consequences of playing this particular game.

Darren rolled his eyes as if he'd expected that reaction. "Come on, it's either this or 'Never Have I Ever.'"

Crosby pictured playing a drinking game with Darren and internally grimaced. "Fine. 'Truth or Dare.'"

"Truth," Darren said promptly.

Well, shit. Now Crosby had to think of a question.

He looked at his temporary roommate, wondering what he could ask that wouldn't give too much away. Darren was about his age, thirty-one. He looked a little older, maybe, his face a sharp collection of angles carved out of light skin, crowned by expressively slashed eyebrows. He had dark, thick hair that in its current style curled luxuriously around his ears, and clear gray eyes with lush lashes. He was dressed casually in a red flannel shirt, jeans, and hiking socks.

Crosby had dressed up for the earlier watch party for the first episode of the new season of *Sawyer's* in taupe slacks and a dark green sweater over a crisp white collared shirt. Now he felt overdressed, but the only clothes he had to change into weren't much better. As a lifelong resident of Manhattan, he kept a change of clothes in his trunk in case of emergencies, like a terrorist attack or last-minute audition. His emergency clothes consisted of black jeans, a green long-sleeved T-shirt, extra socks, a pair of boxers, and a warm black cashmere sweater.

Darren's eyebrows wiggled–impatiently it seemed to Crosby. He settled on a question, if only to fill the silence that kept blooming between them.

"Why aren't you with your family today?" It wasn't the sexiest question he could ask, but that was probably for the best. He should not be thinking about Darren and sex anyway. He sighed before he could help himself.

Darren's forehead wrinkled at Crosby's sigh, but he didn't comment. Instead, he explained, "We're a Chrismukkah family. I already did the Hanukkah thing with my dad a couple of weeks ago. My parents are divorced. Anyway, I'd usually go to my mom's, but she went with her boyfriend to his family in Florida. My brothers are both with their in-laws. Hanging with the Cove crew seemed like a good way to spend Christmas."

Crosby froze as he processed the plethora of new information. He'd technically known Darren for fifteen years, but he didn't know anything about his family. His parents were divorced? He had brothers? Were they older or younger? He swallowed down his follow-up questions because they were playing a game to pass the time, not getting to know each other at a cocktail party.

"Truth or dare?" Darren said, since he was normal.

"Dare," Crosby said, after a moment's hesitation. He glanced around the hundred-square foot room while he waited for Darren to issue a challenge, trying not to question his life choices up to that point. How terrible a dare could he manage to come up with in a hotel room in the middle of a snowstorm on Christmas?

The room itself was nice, but unremarkable. Two

queen beds with cozy white comforters, plenty of pillows, midnight blue accents from the lampshades to the carpet. A big flat screen TV was mounted on the wall across from the beds, over a dresser that hid a fridge with a minibar and the room safe. The adjoining bathroom held a glassed-in shower, low lighting, and copious amounts of the inn's signature toiletry items. The room wasn't the problem. It was sanctuary from the storm, and also a prison, since until the snow stopped and roads cleared, Crosby couldn't leave Misty Harbor to go home to New York.

Darren smirked lightly as he formulated his dare.

Crosby's palms went unaccountably sweaty.

"All right, Crosby. I dare you to go get us some ice."

Crosby frowned, suspicious. That didn't sound so bad.

"In your underwear," Darren finished, a gleeful smirk on his face.

Crosby glared. "Seriously? You want me to get kicked out of the hotel?"

"Oh, come on, they won't kick you out. Probably no one will even see you. Besides, the ice machine is only around the corner. Easy as pie."

Crosby bit his lip. He'd stayed at the inn enough times to know exactly where the ice machine was, in a little alcove around the corner from the elevator bank. It wasn't likely he'd run into anybody on the way. But the dare meant he'd have to strip. In front of Darren. He'd agreed to share close quarters, but taking his clothes off in front of the guy wasn't part of the deal.

Still, he'd agreed to the game, and it was too late to switch to truth. He sighed as loudly as he could and pulled his sweater over his head in one motion. He caught Darren's expression out of the corner of his eye. He looked slightly surprised, and maybe a little impressed, as Crosby continued matter-of-factly stripping.

He undid the flashy gold cufflinks of his French-cuffed shirt, set them on top of the dresser. He unbuttoned the shirt and shrugged it off. He wasn't wearing an undershirt, and the air suddenly felt cool, sharpening his nipples to points. But as an actor, he had to be comfortable being around strangers in various stages of undress, so it wasn't weird to undo his belt and slide off his trousers, though he carefully laid them over the back of a chair so they wouldn't wrinkle. Socks were last. He sat on the bed and reached down to remove them, but Darren stopped him.

"You can leave those on," he said, voice barely hiding a laugh. "I'm not a monster."

"Gee, thanks," Crosby said, standing up in nothing but his socks, black boxer-briefs, and chunky gold-and-silver wristwatch. He felt exposed, and a little cold. "Here I go."

"Wait." Darren darted across the room and grabbed the brown leather ice bucket, thrusting it at Crosby before he got to the door. "You'll need this."

Crosby saw a room key on a ledge by the door and swiped it.

"What, you don't think I'll let you back in?" Darren asked.

"I'm not taking any chances," Crosby said dryly.

Darren grinned. "Smart man."

Crosby steeled himself and left the room before he could back out. He speed-walked to the ice machine, spotting exactly zero other people, and pressed the bar to activate the ice dispenser. Small cubes of ice slowly filled the bucket as he thought about Darren's parting smile. It had seemed more like a smile of solidarity than one making fun of Crosby.

Maybe this wasn't the worst thing in the world. Maybe after this unexpected interlude, he and Darren could actually be friends. Maybe Crosby would finally get over his stupid little crush and be able to see Darren as just another one of his *Sawyer's Cove* castmates, instead of the guy who tied him into knots so tight he could barely interact with him.

He was heading back to the room with the full ice bucket, passing the elevator bank, when one dinged its arrival. He picked up the pace. Half a hallway to go when he heard a couple of chattering young women get off the elevator. Their conversation died down when they caught sight of him from the back, hoofing it down the hallway. He reached the room as he heard the explosion of laughter behind him. He forced himself not to look back. God forbid one of them whipped out her phone and got a shot of his face. He struggled with the key and ice bucket for a long moment, then finally the door opened, and he escaped to safety.

The echoes of the girls' laughter were still ringing in his ears when he shoved the ice bucket into Darren's arms. "Well, that was humiliating," he said, a prickle of heat spreading from his cheeks down his throat.

"Was it?" Darren said, perking up as he stashed the ice bucket on the dresser. "Bonus."

Crosby ignored him, reached for his slacks.

"Hey, you want to borrow some sweats? I have an extra pair. They're clean, I promise." Darren was already rummaging in his open overnight bag.

"Uh."

"Here." Darren held out a pair of dark gray joggers.

For the first time, Crosby realized how close in size they were. Darren was probably an inch taller, but they were both built wiry, with layers of lean muscle over slim bones. Crosby met Darren's gray eyes as he reached for the offering. "Thanks."

"Sure. We're stuck here. Might as well be comfortable. Your turn, by the way."

"Turn?"

"Truth or dare."

Oh, right. The game.

He put on the joggers. He felt better once there was another layer between him and Darren, though it wasn't like Darren had checked him out or anything. Which was a little disappointing, to be honest. Crosby worked out, he had to be in good shape for his job, and he was generally considered attractive, with his classical nose, milky white complexion, full mouth, wide green eyes, and curly blond mop of hair. But Darren hadn't seemed to take more than a cursory glance at his body when he had the chance. Oh, well.

"Truth or dare?"

"Dare," he said. "I like to change it up."

"Okay," Crosby said, looking around the room for inspiration. "Let's put that ice to good use."

Darren frowned at the ice bucket. "How?" he asked suspiciously.

"Stick your hand in the ice, and keep it there for a minute," Crosby said, choosing the first idea that came into his head. "You can pick which hand."

"A minute?" Darren's eyebrows rose.

Crosby second guessed himself. Too long? He didn't want to give the guy frostbite. "Thirty seconds," he amended. Then he smiled evilly. "I'm not a monster."

Darren chuckled, shrugged, and plunged his left hand into the bucket. After a few seconds, he shivered.

"Cold?" Crosby asked mildly.

Darren stuck his tongue out at him. "I hope you're keeping track of the time."

Crosby hadn't been. He'd been enjoying the quasi-fun they were having. He glanced at his watch, counted down twenty ticks of the second hand.

*Close enough.*

"Okay, time's up."

Darren removed his hand to reveal red, wet skin. "Ouch."

Crosby shifted, suddenly regretting that he'd caused Darren pain. He was about to apologize when Darren lunged, clapping his icy cold hand to the back of Crosby's neck. The cold stunned him, but not as much as Darren voluntarily touching him. He gasped and instinctively pulled away, scrambling onto his bed. He cursed and Darren laughed, but not meanly.

"Sorry, I had to," Darren said. "There's something about you that makes the devil on my shoulder go crazy."

Crosby shivered again. A chill still clung to his neck. He hadn't put a shirt on after his trip to the ice machine, and he had goosebumps all over. His nipples were diamond hard.

This time, Darren did glance down Crosby's chest from his position at the foot of Crosby's bed. He was definitely looking, but his expression was unreadable, and he walked quickly to the bathroom. He left the door open while he rinsed his hands in the sink, presumably in warm water.

"Truth or dare?" he called out.

Crosby, disoriented from Darren's touch, glance, and the fact that he was actually having fun, spoke without thinking. "Truth."

# Chapter Two



*Finally*, Darren thought when he heard Crosby's choice.

He'd been half-afraid Crosby, stubborn asshole that he was, would persistently choose dare, and Darren would have to resort to some childish tactic like saying, "I dare you to tell me the truth about..." Sure, two thirty-something men playing Truth or Dare was kind of childish in the first place. But at least Crosby was interacting with him.

Sometimes he felt as if Crosby simply looked right

through him, as if he had a blind spot where Darren was concerned, and instead of seeing a co-worker, he saw empty space. Today was proof they could interact without one of them exploding. On the other hand, that meant all those times Crosby had seemed to glance at him without seeing him, when he'd acted like Darren was invisible, had been Crosby's deliberate choice. Darren had wondered for years about the difficult dynamic between them, and now was his chance to find out.

He leaned against the doorjamb. Crosby was sitting on his bed, giving the impression of a spooked deer, eyes big and body still. He was shirtless, which Darren acknowledged was partly his fault, and not for the first time he concluded it was fortunate Crosby's face resembled a Greek god's, because it made up for his stick-in-the-mud personality.

Though he'd been making an effort tonight, Darren had to admit. He was beginning to think Ariel had been right all those times she told him Crosby was shy in groups, that he was better one-on-one. Darren had never been given the opportunity to be one-on-one with Crosby, so how would he know?

"Why don't you like me?" He felt only mildly embarrassed to be asking such a self-centered question. It was the question he most wanted to know the answer to. Besides, the answer had implications outside of this hotel room, professionally anyway.

He watched Crosby take in the question, observed his shoulders straighten and hands flex. He parted his mouth, that sculpted pink bow that kept millions of fangirls—and more than likely plenty of fanboys, too—up at night since he'd first played Sawyer North, the foundational character of *Sawyer's Cove*, fifteen years ago.

"I—" Crosby started and stopped immediately.

"Come on, it's not rocket science," Darren said, suddenly wishing he'd asked something else, some innocuous question about Crosby's porn habits or something.

"I don't not like you," Crosby said.

Darren curled his lip derisively. "Yeah, right."

"It's true," Crosby said quietly.

"What kind of answer is that? You don't not like me? Then why—"

"You had your turn," Crosby said, breaking in. "Truth or dare?"

"I'm not going to play if you're going to cheat," Darren said, feeling like he was missing something and also rubbed raw with the familiar irritation of Crosby always seeming to know something he didn't.

"Fine." Crosby bit his fat bottom lip. "You can have another turn."

Darren grabbed the remote and turned on the TV, sick of the awkward silences. The hotel's welcome screen came on, and he quickly flipped through the channels, seeking a distraction.

"Truth or dare?" he said, keeping his gaze on the screen.

"Are we playing or watching TV?" Crosby said, sounding annoyed.

Good. Darren was annoyed, too. He sat on the end of his bed and skipped through the channels quickly, not sure what he was looking for.

"Truth," Crosby said when Darren didn't answer.

Darren flashed past weather, sports, and infomercials before he stumbled on *White Christmas*. Rosemary Clooney was being offered a late-night snack of liverwurst and buttermilk by Bing Crosby. He turned the volume down so low he could barely hear it, but that didn't matter. He had the entire movie memorized, anyway.

"Why do you go by 'Crosby?'" he asked, eyes trained on the television, his voice carefully flat, as if he couldn't care less about the answer, since Crosby probably wouldn't answer anyway.

"I hate the name Spencer," Crosby said, scorn in his voice. "Sounds like a prep school drug dealer."

Darren let out a small, surprised laugh, but he kept his attention on the screen. Maybe if he didn't look at Crosby, he'd keep talking.

"Crosby's my middle name, my mom's maiden name. I dropped the Van Wyck when I first started booking jobs. Looking back, all the casting people knew who I was anyway, but I was young and naive enough to think I was getting cast on my own. Who knows? Maybe it helped. Spencer Crosby sounds marginally less like a nepo baby than Spencer Van Wyck, son of Tony winner Daniel Van Wyck, right?"

Darren absorbed that. He knew Crosby's dad was Daniel Van Wyck. Everyone did, or at least in acting circles. He thought about how he'd assumed it meant Crosby had an advantage, but then he recognized Crosby wouldn't see it that way. He'd see it as a stumbling block in his career, not a boon.

The movie went to a commercial, and Darren muted the TV. Still, he kept his body facing the screen instead of turning toward Crosby. He didn't want to scare him out of this genuine conversation.

"This industry is built on nepotism. It's just that no one would recognize Darren Silverstein as the son of Lou Silverstein, first AD on *Murder at the Museum Three*. You can't help your dad being one of the most famous stage actors of his generation."

"Your dad's an AD?"

Darren listened hard, but he couldn't detect any snobbery in the question, only curiosity.

"Yep. Thirty years. Mostly low-budget stuff. My mom was a casting director before she started teaching high school drama. And hey, at least you have talent. A famous actor parent isn't a guarantee you can act. Believe me, I've heard all the stories from my mom."

"You think I have talent?" This time, the simple curiosity in Crosby's voice seemed to mask something else.

Darren lifted a shoulder carelessly. "You're okay." It wasn't his job to stroke Spencer Crosby's ego. He twisted his head a few degrees to catch Crosby's reaction in his peripheral vision. He was wearing a small, pleased smile.

Darren suddenly felt like a jerk. Crosby could be standoffish and stiff and almost offensively sealed off. He was probably an introvert, and just because Darren was a people person, didn't mean social situations came easily to everyone. He was an actor; he knew how easy it was to start doubting how good you were, no matter how many parts you scored.

"I loved *Over Easy*," he said, keeping his voice casual. "Great show, and you were really good."

"You saw it?"

Darren had seen the off-Broadway production twice, in fact. At the time, it hadn't even occurred to him to let Crosby know he'd be in the audience. They weren't friends, after all.

"Was the play hard? I haven't done live theater since middle school."

"I love theater," Crosby said. "It's terrifying and exhilarating."

"The adoring applause doesn't hurt either."

Crosby didn't answer. Darren forgot about the movie and turned, scooting farther up the bed to face his roommate. He looked a little upset, and again, Darren felt like a jerk.

"I didn't mean it like that. Anyone would appreciate the instant gratification, wouldn't they?"

"Sure." Crosby shrugged, but he seemed shuttered, the edges of his mouth turned down.

"So what are you going to be in next?" Darren

wouldn't normally ask an actor about their upcoming projects, in case they didn't have any, but work seemed to be the only subject they had in common.

"You don't have to do this," Crosby said.

"Huh?"

"We don't have to make conversation just because you have social anxiety if you can't win everyone over."

"Excuse me?" What the hell did that mean?

"You always make friends with everyone on set. You need people to like you. You're obsessed with it—you think I don't like you, and it's been bothering you for years—am I right? Give up."

Darren felt a flare of anger, and then–just as quickly–it subsided, a rueful acceptance left in its wake. "You got me there. I do want everyone to like me. Does that make me a criminal?"

"No. You're lucky, because making friends is easy for you."

He heard the implication in Crosby's statement. Making friends wasn't easy for *him*.

Darren flashed back to the first time he'd laid eyes on Spencer Crosby. He was sitting in his mom's living room to watch *Sawyer's Cove*, the show everyone was buzzing about, a young actor himself, both looking forward to and scared of his future in an unforgiving industry. He'd watched this impossibly beautiful boy walk on screen like he was born to be there. His hero worship of the actor who played Sawyer North had lasted until he'd landed his own part on the show and made it to his first table read. He and Crosby didn't have any scenes together, but he couldn't help taking it personally when Crosby seemed to go out of his way to avoid him on set and off.

They say never meet your heroes.

Maybe he'd taken Crosby's indifference too personally. Maybe it didn't have anything to do with Darren.

Maybe they could start over.

"I grew up around my dad and his filmmaker friends," he said slowly. Crosby's defiant expression didn't alter with the change in subject. "I begged him to take me to sets with him when I was little, and I found it all so fascinating. Everyone had these super specific jobs, and if they didn't do the best they could, the entire production could go haywire. It was so exciting when I was a kid. I wanted to be on those sets more than I wanted to be at school or with my friends. Eventually, I convinced my parents to let me try acting. I had a leg up because my casting director mom knew how to coach me for auditions, and my dad had given me a chance to see how it all worked behind the scenes. I feel comfortable around the crew, on sets. And yeah, it helps that I'm a naturally friendly guy. I wish you'd—"

He stopped. It didn't matter. He swerved. "I've been directing some TV."

"Yeah?" Crosby looked at his feet instead of at Darren.

Darren scooted to the edge of his bed. "Yeah. I put a bee in Selena's ear about hiring me to direct a *Sawyer's Cove* episode next season."

"Oh," Crosby said flatly.

"That's not going to be a problem for you, is it?" he asked carefully.

"Why would it be a problem for me?" Crosby got up before Darren could answer and put on the soft green sweater he'd been wearing earlier. It seemed almost like he was donning armor to get through the conversation.

"I don't know," Darren said, losing patience. He was trying to make a connection here. "Maybe it would be an issue for you, the way my entire existence seems to be an issue for you. And I know what you said, you 'don't not' like me, which is a truckload of bullshit. I know you think I need to be liked, and maybe that's true, but I can take it if you tell me the truth. I'm an adult; I can handle it."

"There's nothing to tell." Crosby worried his plump bottom lip between his perfectly straight white teeth. "Drop it. You're going to direct *Sawyer's Cove*. Awesome. I'll bet you're fantastic at it. It'll be great." His monotone betrayed no excitement whatsoever at the prospect.

This was ridiculous. Clearly, there was something wrong and Crosby was a big liar.

"Look, I'm only going to say this one time, because it's going to bother me if I don't. Is it because I'm gay?"

"Jesus."

Crosby sat back down on the bed and crossed his arms over his sweater-covered chest. He took a deep breath. Darren could see his chest moving up and down deliberately under the soft, dark green material. Crosby lifted his head and stared directly at Darren.

"In a way."

Darren's heart seized up. Shit. He'd always suspected the reason Crosby had never warmed up to him was that he was uncomfortable with him being gay, but he hadn't wanted to fully acknowledge it, for some reason. It's not like he'd never experienced homophobia. Being out in Hollywood was a lot harder when he started than it was now, and it still wasn't a walk in the park. But hearing Crosby say it hurt more than he thought it would.

He stood up, wanting to escape, but there was nowhere to escape to. It was dark and snowing outside. He could have gone to the lobby, but why should he have to retreat when Crosby was the one who—

"I'm gay, too," Crosby said, staring at his socks again. "When I was a teenager, I was really in denial about it. Like, serious denial. It's taken me about ten years of therapy to even say those words out loud. And you showed up to set, all cocky and daring the world to take issue with you. So unafraid. So certain of who you were. And I was jealous."

He sighed and scrubbed a hand over his face tiredly. "It turned me into an asshole. Or, more of an asshole than I already was. I was seventeen. I was a jerk. I still am, probably. But it was totally unfair of me to treat you the way I did just because I was insecure."

Crosby finally made eye contact with him, and Darren's spine buzzed.

"This is about a decade and a half overdue, but I apologize."

Fifteen years of wondering what exactly he'd done to make Crosby hate him suddenly flipped, as if his memories had been spun through a blender and he was seeing all of their interactions again, for the first time.

"Fuck." He'd never suspected internalized homophobia was the culprit.

"Yeah." Crosby sounded sad.

"I wish I'd known." He didn't know what else to say.

"I didn't—I don't like to mix my personal life and my work life."

"Cool, cool," Darren said quickly, still dazed as if Crosby had swung a two-by-four at his head and he was hallucinating cartoon birds flying in a circle around him.

He was thinking about all the weird little interactions between them on and off set, how Crosby had seemed to sneer at Darren's moments of flamboyance. He didn't present as overtly queer, but he had his moments. Crosby, on the other hand, had seemed to box himself into this very rigid role of the stereotypical standoffish leading man. If he was shy to start with and then battling his own denial about his sexuality, well, no wonder he was hard to get close to.

"So I hope you do get to direct *Sawyer's Cove*. Your episode of *Vampire Brothers* was the best of the whole season."

"Wait—you know I've been directing?"

"Uh. Yeah."

Darren shook his head, as if the motion would cause all the preconceived notions he'd had crowbarred loose to fit back into place and make sense again.

"I'm sorry if I made you feel—I didn't handle any of that very well," Crosby said.

"It's okay," Darren said gently. "Are you out now?"

"I've been out for a while to my family and my close friends. My agent and my manager know, of course. It's not a secret, I guess. I never wanted to make some formal statement."

"Okay."

The adrenaline rush of the conversation drained away, leaving Darren exhausted. He stifled a yawn but couldn't entirely hide it from Crosby, who smirked. The familiar expression now seemed forced, rather than his default.

"Bedtime?" Crosby asked.

"I guess." The movie was ending, and he flicked off the screen.

Darren felt unaccountably sad. His image of Crosby as this perfectly sculpted, perfectly snobby, perfectly unapproachable statue was crumbling, and now he was seeing him for what he was—flesh and blood. Crosby was only a guy, an uncommonly good-looking guy, but a guy nonetheless, who had as much heart and soul as the next person.

He felt cheated of the years they could have spent actually being friends. And not because he needed everyone to like him. This wasn't about that. Well, not entirely.

He looked at Crosby now and saw not a statue, but the seventeen-year-old kid he'd been when Darren first met him. He wished he'd been able to see that Crosby's attitude was as much an act as the way he played brooding, over-analytical Sawyer. He wished he could go back and try harder to befriend seventeen-year-old Crosby. Maybe things would have been less painful for the guy if he'd had a friend who knew, at least in part, what he was going through as he navigated the choppy waters of growing up, coming out, and becoming famous all at the same time.

He got off the bed and went to the bathroom. He'd brush his teeth and go to sleep, and maybe in the morning they could start fresh. He was an optimist. He'd always appreciated fresh starts.

He turned around in the doorway. "I'm sorry I wasn't there for you back then. I wish I had been."

Darren didn't think Crosby was going to say anything, but then—"I wish I'd let you."

Darren shot him a small smile, and the door between them closed with a *click*.

# Chapter Three



Crosby's heart pumped like he was on mile twenty-five of a marathon. It thundered in his chest, driving overly hot blood throughout his body. He stared at the closed bathroom door for a solid minute before rousing himself to get as ready for sleep as he could.

He set his water bottle on the bedside table, took out his allergy medicine, swallowed a pill automatically, all while his brain was racing with what he'd just done. He'd finally come out to Darren Silverstein, and the world hadn't ended.

He hadn't been lying. His being gay wasn't a secret. If anyone had been paying attention the past few years, they would have noticed he'd stopped bringing female dates to any functions, unless they were friends, like when he brought Ariel Tulip to the *Over Easy* cast party.

He'd even gotten involved at Rainbow Canyon, the LGBTQ+ nonprofit, where his co-worker Nash Speedwell spent a lot of time and money. More recently, he'd asked his agent to find him parts for queer characters, something he'd never done before. He had an audition on New Year's Eve for a movie called *Dessert First*. The main character, Grady, was gay, and Crosby was gunning for the part harder than usual. He was ready to see if playing a gay character was somehow going to feel more authentic than any of the other characters he'd played.

But not being in the closet wasn't the same thing as being out.

Darren was *out*. He talked about being a gay actor and director in interviews, and he'd played mostly gay characters since he started acting. His character on *Sawyer's Cove* was iconic—he played Noah Rosen, the love interest of Nash's character, Will, for two and a half seasons, and their romance was the most functional one on the entire show.

So, he hadn't been worried about coming out to Darren. He'd been surprisingly subdued about the reveal anyway.

No, mostly Crosby was mourning the loss of one of the layers of protection he had when it came to his crush. If Darren didn't know Crosby was gay, then he couldn't interpret any of the weird, pathetic things Crosby did as having anything to do with his real secret —he'd had a thing for Darren for years.

Usually, he felt lighter after he told someone the truth about his sexuality. And he did feel lighter now, in a way. But there was a new buzzing under his skin—the awareness that with one layer peeled away, the other, more dangerous truth was closer to being revealed.

Crosby almost wanted to shout it out and get it over with, instead of this slow peeling back of their antagonism toward each other. Darren would never hate him because he was gay, but how would he react if Crosby told him exactly how much he "didn't not like" him?

He sighed and pulled down the sheets on his bed. He was suddenly tired, shocked it was so late when he checked the time.

Darren emerged from the bathroom, and they switched places. Crosby brushed his teeth and splashed water on his face, while Darren moved around in the bedroom. It was a strange dance, echoing the motions of a couple getting ready for bed. Only, they weren't sharing one, thank goodness. Darren was merely doing him a favor by giving him a place to shelter from the storm.

As he looked at himself in the mirror, missing the comfort of his own nightly routine, Crosby felt homesick for the city, for his quiet, orderly Chelsea apartment. As a New York-based actor who did a lot of theater and some movies and TV sprinkled in, he traveled often for work. He'd spent the majority of the fall right there in

Misty Harbor, in a little rental cottage a ways outside of town. He was no stranger to hotel rooms and being on the road. But right now, he'd give anything to be at home, wrapped in his ultra-warm fleece blanket, watching one of his comfort movies. Alone.

He might be out of the storm, but he didn't exactly feel safe.

Maybe it being Christmas made him extra nostalgic. Darren hadn't asked, but his parents were in London for the holidays this year. His dad was in previews for a play scheduled to open in the new year. His mom went where his father went. They'd made some effort to get him to come over; London at Christmastime was a festive time. But with *Sawyer's Cove* debuting and everyone planning to get together to watch it, he'd decided to stay home. As much as he protested all the buddy-buddy, decidedly un-Hollywood camaraderie of the Cove crew, he enjoyed being part of it.

He dried his already dry hands one more time. He couldn't stall any longer. He had to go out there and get some sleep, and in the morning the snow would have stopped, and he could make his escape. He and Darren wouldn't have to see each other again until next season's production. And after this ice breaker of an experience, they wouldn't be so prickly around each other.

Maybe by being friends, Crosby's attraction to Darren would lessen. Perhaps he'd be able to look at him without a stomach full of angry butterflies someday.

He left the bathroom. Darren was propped up on pillows in bed. Reading a book. Shirtless.

He swallowed against a lump of his heart trying to escape through his throat. He blinked stupidly at the image of a beautiful man reading in bed and resisted the urge to climb in with him. What would Darren do if he crawled onto the bed, pushed the book down, and kissed him?

The improbability of that ever happening in a million years made him snort. The inelegant noise in the small space broke the spell. Darren glanced up, following him with his gaze as Crosby moved around to the other bed and got in, still wearing all his layers. He'd probably be sweating all night, but he couldn't handle getting naked with Darren watching him again.

"Your phone dinged," Darren said, breaking the uncomfortable silence between them.

"What are you reading?" Crosby asked as he got up to unplug his phone from the charger by the TV and bring it back to bed with him.

"A biography of Mike Nichols," Darren said.

"The director?"

"He's a hero of mine."

"Cool."

It was kind of unbearably impressive that Darren had begun directing. He wondered if he was more serious on his own set than he was on the *Sawyer's Cove* set, where he always seemed to be making jokes or pulling good-natured pranks.

Darren turned a page, and Crosby read his texts.

TREVOR

> I finished watching the first two
> episodes. I'm crying. They were so
> good. You were so good. I'm
> hyperventilating. Not really. I'll be okay.

He couldn't suppress a chuckle at Trevor's character-istic histrionics. But he was glad he liked the show. In his escape from the storm, he'd almost forgotten the show would be eliciting reactions from fans. He tried not to read reviews, and his social media presence was lack-luster at best, but he knew it mattered if people liked it. Trevor was a superfan who knew half the cast and crew personally from waiting on them at the Misty Harbor Bakeshop, so he wasn't exactly an objective voice. Still, it was nice to hear.

Trevor had followed up with another text.

> Is New York getting hit with as much
> snow as us? We're supposed to get,
> like, a foot and a half.

Shit. He tapped out his reply quickly.

> I'm actually in Misty Harbor, stuck here
> because of the storm. Glad you liked
> the show. I only saw the first episode,
> but I thought it was good.

He switched over to his other messages.

ARIEL

> Have you killed each other yet?

> Jay and Cami have a couch if you need it.

He answered her briefly.

> We're both still alive.

By which time, Trevor had responded.

> OMG are you at the inn? Stay off the roads!!

The kid was quite a mother-hen.

> I am and I will.

> How did you get a room? I heard they were all full.

Crosby chuckled. Of course he'd heard. Trevor heard everything that happened in Misty Harbor. He glanced at Darren, who was staring intently at the page he was reading. He knew giving any information to Trevor was like spray painting the news in neon on the stone facade of the Misty Harbor library in the center of town, but he liked being able to share something of his life with a true friend.

> Darren had an extra bed.

The answer came after a short pause.

You're shacking up with Darren Silverstein?? Noah Rosen?? OMG I haven't met him yet. Is he nice?

Don't tell me if he isn't.

He reflected for a moment. Darren, despite the fact that Crosby seemed to bring out the salty side of him, was nice. And of course Trevor would be enamored with him. Trevor, like many a young queer man hungry for representation, had latched onto the openly gay characters in *Sawyer's Cove* with a passion. Crosby, playing iconically straight, and straight-laced, and sometimes toxically fuckboyish Sawyer, was no one's role model.

Nash got to play Will, gaining accolades for portraying a nuanced and empowered gay character, while Crosby had the role of a cis straight white boy. He was realizing how much that had begun to bother him over the years.

Not that Crosby was itching to be anyone's hero. But by disappearing into, or behind, Sawyer North, he could avoid having to share anything really authentic about himself with their audience.

Trevor had seen through that the first time they met. He'd been so petrified with joy at interacting with him and Nash that Crosby had found himself opening up, if only to put the kid more at ease. Trevor had looked at him, and after his initial shock wore off, had seen someone trying to be himself who wasn't exactly sure how. Trevor, who wore makeup and long hair and a rainbow friendship bracelet around his knobby wrist, had immediately taught him something about being himself.

> Darren is nice. I'll tell him you say hi.

Trevor responded back with an unintelligible keyboard smash, which Crosby assumed was the end of the conversation for now. He laughed lightly again as he put his phone on the nightstand and tried to get comfortable in the bed.

"Was that your boyfriend?" Darren asked without looking up from the book.

Crosby felt his mouth fall open like a character in a cartoon. "Huh?" he said intelligently.

"I was just wondering who could make you laugh like that," Darren said, sounding supremely uninterested in the answer to his own question.

*Like what?* Crosby wanted to ask. He'd barely laughed at all. But he supposed he was wary about laughing in the presence of Darren. He'd trained himself to police his actions and reactions around the guy, lest he give something away.

Suddenly, he felt exhausted by all the pretense and playacting. Crosby had spent way too much of his life obsessing over Darren, afraid to be himself. He was sick of it all.

He supposed this entire night was about letting go of those feelings, those old insecurities he'd used like a crutch, or a shield for far too long.

"No, a friend," he said belatedly. "I don't have a

boyfriend," he added on, because wasn't that what Darren was really asking?

"Oh. Good. I mean, not *good*. Cool. Whatever." Darren turned the page quickly, and Crosby had to smile. It was nice seeing Darren something other than perfectly together.

"What about you?" Crosby asked, feeling bold. "Boyfriend?"

"What, are we still playing 'Truth or Dare?'" Darren said, the snarkiness returning.

Instantly stung, Crosby drew back, but Darren backtracked quickly. "Sorry, that was shitty. I'm tired." He put the book aside and rubbed his eyes. "No boyfriend."

"Okay." He tried to tell himself it hadn't been a mistake to ask.

"Okay," Darren said, turning on his side to face Crosby. The only light in the room came from the reading lamp above his bed, and he reached up and clicked it off, instantly dousing the room in darkness.

Crosby closed his eyes. It was just as dark inside his head. Black and blessedly empty. He was normally quick to fall asleep, quick to wake up. Tonight, the heaviness of sleep came on a little slower than usual, interrupted when Darren's voice came quietly out of the dark.

"Goodnight, Crosby."

"Goodnight."

# Chapter Four



His bed was made of rocks.

Darren twisted his spine until it popped satisfyingly. He didn't remember the bed being this uncomfortable the previous night, but maybe he just hadn't noticed. He couldn't get comfortable. He was too hot, even wearing only his boxers to bed, as he normally did.

He couldn't stop the stream of thoughts that had been running through his head since he'd seen Crosby stare at his phone and laugh privately at something he'd read there. He'd been watching him out of the corner of his eye while he pretended to read his book, astonished when he saw an unguarded expression cross Crosby's face.

A genuine smile made him look so different—boyishly handsome rather than sterilely beautiful. Darren had experienced a disorienting moment of pure want. He wanted to put a smile like that on Crosby's face.

Twelve hours ago, he would have said that was one bucket list item he'd never manage to cross off. But now, if he could stay out of his own way and they could let a friendship spring up in the absence of their silly mutual dislike, it might happen one day.

Darren had suddenly been blindingly jealous of the person on the other side of that phone screen, and it unsettled him. He and Crosby were only barely communicating—he'd be the biggest cliche in the world if the moment he discovered he and Crosby played for the same team, he started thinking of him as a prospect.

He shook his head and turned over in the hotel bed that had somehow been replaced by a mattress of cactus paddles.

With a frustrated huff, he kicked the covers off and sat up. Crosby was an unmoving lump on the other bed, still as a corpse. Darren felt his ire rise again. Of course, *he* slept like a baby, while Darren chased his thoughts around in circles in his brain.

What was it with this guy? Why did Darren care so much? He wasn't delusional—he didn't actually need to be best friends with every single person he met. But there was something about Crosby that brushed him the wrong way, like he was one of those sequin-studded sweaters his niece liked to wear. When you brushed the sequins down, they were one color, then you brushed them up, and another color was revealed. Crosby was brushing against his sequins, and Darren didn't like it.

He got out of bed quietly. If he turned his phone on, it would be hours before he'd be able to sleep, and he didn't want to turn the lamp on to go back to his book. Instead, he crossed to the window and pushed aside the heavy blackout curtain.

Outside, the world was one giant Swarovski crystal. Crosby would have liked the analogy. Darren had noticed Crosby liked a bit of bling, if his ostentatious watch and polished silver sports car were any indication. Somewhere down there, his beater of a Jeep was getting snowed in by glistening white snow. Crosby's two-seater was probably going to take forever to dig out.

It was magical, the entire world buffeted and blanketed in a rare early snowstorm. Last year, they'd barely gotten any snow all winter. It was nice to know a white Christmas could still be had once in a while.

He looked out the window a little longer, his soul calming. He didn't know what to do with his changing feelings toward Crosby, but he decided he felt hopeful about the morning. Maybe they could put the last years of antagonism behind them for good.

He tiptoed back to bed, and when he lay down this time, the mattress had gotten much more comfortable.

·  ·  ·

When Darren opened his eyes next, he thought he was dreaming. Someone was standing in the very spot where he'd stood last night, gazing out the window. Gray light framed the figure, and Darren had to blink a few times until the backlit shape resolved itself into a man.

Spencer Crosby.

He had his back to the room, and what a back it was. Sometime in the night, he'd removed his sweater and the joggers. He must have been hot, too. Darren was sweltering under the heavy hotel sheets.

Crosby stood in nothing but skintight black boxer briefs like a moody underwear model, sharp shoulder blades pointing to his elegantly curved spine. Darren hadn't let himself notice during the ice machine dare, but Crosby's ass was full and round, accentuating muscular thighs and his trim waist.

His face had been likened to a Greek sculpture by more than one effusive entertainment journalist, but his body could have been carved out of marble just as easily. Defensively, Darren put his hand on his belly. He'd always been skinny, but not like Crosby, where the muscle was only a layer away. Darren was lanky, but soft. He'd never gotten into gym culture. In the Will-Noah relationship, Noah was the one with the muscles, and Noah was the slender twink. Of course, that had been when they were all much younger. He'd be thirty-two soon. His more athletic friends had been campaigning for him to take up pickleball for cardio and stress relief. He was thinking about it.

As he watched Crosby at the window, he realized

what he wanted more than anything was to give their relationship a fresh start. Despite not killing each other the previous evening, they weren't exactly friends. He should probably let it go; it didn't matter if they were friends or not.

But he didn't want to let it go.

He was stubborn, but Crosby was clearly more so. And Darren actually liked him. They both lived in New York, though Darren didn't know exactly where in the city Crosby hung his hat. Maybe when they got back, they could hang out. They didn't have to confine their interactions to *Sawyer's Cove*-sanctioned events.

Crosby turned away from the window, letting the curtain fall back into place. Before the morning light was completely blocked, his face was illuminated, and Darren was shocked by the sad look on his face.

What did Crosby have to be sad about? He was a successful actor. The *Sawyer's Cove* reboot was clearly going to be a hit. Being the main character in a culturally important, commercially successful TV show wasn't enough for the guy?

But that line of thinking was the old Darren. He didn't know as much as he thought about Crosby, after all. He pushed himself up on his elbows and squinted at Crosby as he rummaged in the bag he'd had with him when he showed up at Darren's door last night.

"Hey."

Crosby whipped his head around. "Hey." It was hard to tell in the dark, but did Crosby's gaze drop to Darren's chest before coming back to eye level? "Um, I'm going to take a shower."

"Okay. I'll order some breakfast."

"Thanks. Order me an omelet, please." Crosby disappeared into the bathroom with a handful of clothes.

Darren flicked on the lamp over his bed, reached for the phone. See, this could work. They were being perfectly civil. Being friends couldn't be long behind.

"No, you are so wrong—it's not even funny," Darren said around his mouthful of hash browns.

"Are you high? There's no way your favorite *Mission: Impossible* can be the second one. It's categorically the worst film in the franchise." Crosby slathered more jam on his toast. They were each sitting on their bed, the room service cart between them as if they were at a trendy Manhattan brunch spot.

"You probably think the first one is the best," Darren said.

"No, you don't get to deflect. How can you possibly defend *Mission: Impossible 2*?"

"John Woo. Slo mo. Hans Zimmer meets Metallica. Tom Cruise free climbing a mountain in a tank top." Darren ticked off his points on his fingers. "What's not to like?"

Crosby shook his head dolefully. Darren hid his smile by sipping from his white porcelain cup of coffee. He was trying to be good, but it was so fun to rile Crosby up. His cheekbones got these really cute streaks of pink, as if there was a sunset reflecting off his perfect skin.

Darren almost choked on his coffee when he realized he was thinking about Crosby's cheekbones. He wanted to get along with the guy, but he didn't want to confuse the matter by allowing any seeds of attraction to grow. Nope, any natural response to Crosby's undeniable aesthetic appeal needed to stay firmly tamped down. If any seedlings sprouted up, Darren resolved to tear them out and throw them on the compost pile of his feelings. He couldn't afford to screw up this detente by crushing on Crosby. There were too many possible negative consequences—not the least of which involved Darren's career.

"Besides, while the first film is the purest, you can't beat Tom Cruise scaling the side of the tallest building in the world with a sandstorm approaching behind him."

"That was pretty sick," Darren allowed. "Fine. But you probably haven't seen the second movie in years. Give me two hours, and I'll change your mind, I promise."

Crosby snorted. "I highly doubt that."

"Come on, there's no movie you like that everyone else thinks is garbage?"

That stopped Crosby. "There's no accounting for taste," he said evasively.

Darren was about to demand titles, but a knock on the door interrupted them. He and Crosby exchanged a glance.

"You expecting someone?"

Crosby shook his head. Since Darren was closest to the door, he got up and answered it. An inn employee was holding what looked like an old-fashioned wicker basket.

"Delivery."

Darren took the basket, mystified. He grabbed a bill out of his wallet and traded it for the basket. The employee smiled her thanks and left.

He held the delivery up once the door had closed behind him. "You order a picnic?"

"I'm still eating breakfast," Crosby said, sounding as confused as Darren.

He lifted the lid and found a note.

*Crosby & Darren,*
*A little something to get you through the storm.*
*Trevor (and Zelda)*

He read the note, and Crosby's expression cleared.

"Who are Trevor and Zelda?" Darren asked. They sounded like characters from an urban fantasy novel.

Crosby slid off the bed and crowded next to Darren so he could see into the basket. He reached in and pulled out a brown bakery box. "Trevor is my friend. He's a local, and he works at the Misty Harbor Bakeshop. Zelda is his boss. And we're lucky." He opened the box, and the aroma of buttery pastry hit Darren's nose, making his mouth water, even though he was full from his eggs.

"Nice friend," Darren said. "What else?"

Crosby laughed as he pulled out the colorful square cardboard box that had been beneath the bakery box. "Battleship!"

Darren laughed, too. "Wow, I guess he knows you like games."

"Yeah. And look, a pack of cards. You play poker?"

Darren shrugged. He'd gone through a poker phase but gave it up when it felt like he was getting too aggro about it. "I've been known to play."

"What's this?" Crosby took the last item out of the basket, something soft, wrapped in white tissue paper. He took off the paper and revealed two pairs of waterproof mittens. He looked up, eyes dancing.

"What are those for?" Darren asked, mystified.

"I think Trevor thinks we should have a snowball fight," Crosby said, sounding delighted. "I don't have my snow gloves with me, so these are perfect."

Darren laughed and set down the now-empty basket. He swept past Crosby to look out the window again. It had continued to snow all morning, and the frozen crystal dreamscape he'd seen late last night was now a full-on winter wonderland, over a foot of snow covering everything they could see, icing the evergreens in the woods behind the inn like powdered sugar on Christmas cookies.

Crosby joined him at the window. "Wow. That's a lot of snow."

All they needed was the sun to come out, and it would be a blindingly perfect setting for an epic snowball fight.

He and Crosby exchanged a glance. It was weird sharing something like this with a guy who, until recently, Darren wouldn't have been surprised to see a picture of in the dictionary next to "party pooper."

"Think it'll stop soon?" Crosby asked. "I don't have proper snow gear."

"Me either." Darren had only planned to spend a couple of nights in Misty Harbor, and the storm had been predicted to miss the area when he left on Christmas Eve. "Just a jacket and hat."

"And gloves," Crosby noted.

"Let's give it a little longer," Darren suggested. "Maybe they'll shovel the walk and we can check it out later."

"Okay," Crosby said. "What should we do until then?"

As he considered the question, Darren noticed how close they were, standing elbow to elbow at the window. He could smell the inn's conditioner in Crosby's still-damp curls and felt how soft Crosby's sweater was when it grazed his arm. Darren choked back the first thought that came to his head, which was that they could pass the time working off their energy in another way.

No, he chided himself. *Dirty thoughts go away.*

He turned to give himself some space, and his gaze landed on the game and deck of cards. "Poker or Battleship?" he asked.

Crosby grinned, and they spoke in unison.

"Battleship."

# Chapter Five

@sawyerscovedaily Oh, Amy and Parker my loves. Parker's bar looks a heckuva lot like Jay Orlando's real life bar...coincidence? I think not. Actually, I know not. They shot it in his bar. #sawyerscove #thecovebar #episode1

After each winning a game of Battleship, splitting the apple turnovers and cranberry muffins between them, and calling down to the desk to ask about the state of the walkways, they were preparing to venture into the outside world.

Darren layered up while Crosby texted Trevor to thank him for the care package.

You didn't have to do that, but it was awesome. Thanks.

He had boots, at least, his go-to winter-in-the-city boots that held up to ice, snow, rain, and general city street gunk. He was lacing them up when Trevor's reply came.

> Don't mention it! If they plow our street, I might come over to visit. My mom is deep in her traditional Boxing Day monster movie marathon and I'm so bored. You're not leaving today, right?

Crosby had been so caught up in finding ways to pass the time with Darren, he hadn't been thinking about when he could return to the city. It felt good to hang out without an agenda. Life in the city was usually rushing from one place to another. On location shoots, like the one for *Sawyer's Cove,* there was often more downtime, but he liked to stay connected to the head-space of his character.

He was glad he still had the ability to let the hours slip by and not worry about what he was supposed to be doing next. The storm combined with that lost time between Christmas and New Year's where normal business was suspended, added to the feeling of being separated from regular life. And partly, it was Darren.

Crosby had begun to let his guard down last night, and when he woke up that morning feeling oddly rested, it had seemed easier to pretend they'd gotten over whatever awkwardness lingered between them and skip to the part where they could enjoy each other's company without second guessing or reading into every tiny interaction.

> Not certain when I'm leaving. I'll let you know. Say hi to your mom for me.

"Are you sure this guy isn't into you?" Darren asked as they got into their outer layers and left the room for the first time in almost twenty-four hours.

"Who, Trevor?"

"Yeah, I mean, he sent you a basket of things he knows you like. Kinda seems into you."

Darren's voice was irritatingly neutral, but Crosby considered the question seriously as they waited for the elevator.

"Trevor is just really...exuberant," Crosby said. "He's not afraid to show his enthusiasm for things. He doesn't see the point in being cagey. I don't think he's into me. I think he has a crush on literally everyone he meets, in a way. He finds something to like in absolutely everyone."

"Even you?" Darren said, nudging Crosby's side and walking into the elevator car.

A day ago, Crosby would have assumed Darren was getting a dig in, but now he could take the gentle teasing for what it was. Growth.

"Even me," he said, letting a smile creep into his voice. He punched the button for the lobby.

"That's cool. But don't be surprised if he asks you out."

"We've gone out as friends. But he's too young for me. He's, like, twenty-two."

"Really," Darren said slyly, "so you're into older guys? Interesting."

"I didn't say that," Crosby said defensively, not sure how the conversation had taken this turn. They emerged into the mostly empty lobby. "I remember what I was like at that age. I was a clueless baby. Too much work."

"But fun. All that stamina." Darren grinned.

Crosby shook his head. Talking about guys with Darren should have been awkward, and it was, but only because Crosby was awkward with everyone about this stuff. Huh. Maybe he was getting over his crush. Maybe being exposed to Darren as a real person instead of just an avatar to put all of Crosby's hidden desires was taking the air out of their dynamic, leaving room for a real friendship to form.

"Hey, let's get you a key while we're here," Darren said, walking over to the reception desk without waiting for Crosby.

A key? It took Crosby the entire length of the lobby to realize Darren meant a key to his room. *Their* room.

"Hiya, Max," Darren said.

Crosby nodded at the familiar man behind the desk. He was a fixture at the Misty Harbor Inn.

"What can I do for you, Mr. Silverstein?" Max asked.

"If we can trust the weather app, we're not getting out of here before tomorrow," Darren said. "I was supposed to check out today, but—"

Max smiled. "I had a feeling you'd want to extend your stay. You and Mr. Crosby are all set for another night."

"Great. Can we get another—" Darren didn't have to finish the sentence, because Max held up a key and passed it to Crosby, with a flourish. "You're a lifesaver. Thanks, Max."

"Anytime." Max looked between them and said, "I hope you're enjoying your stay. It's always a pleasure to host Mr. Orlando's friends."

There was a funny tone in his voice. Max was his usual friendly self, but did he seem particularly happy? Crosby shrugged it off, zipped the key into the pocket of his jacket.

Darren said, "Oh yeah, if you have to be stuck somewhere to ride out a Christmas snowstorm, might as well be here. After all these years, it's like a home away from home."

"Can we quote you on the website?" A plump fifty-something woman in a brown skirt and cream-colored blouse joined Max on the other side of the registration desk.

"Deb, you are a sight for sore eyes," Darren said, winking at Jay Orlando's mom, who happened to be the assistant manager of the inn. "How was your Christmas?"

She grinned at him. "It was lovely, except for the last-minute snowstorm and having to turn away customers in need. Luckily, a big group here for the holidays left today, so we're not so tight on availability. I could probably find another room for you if you need it."

It hadn't occurred to Crosby to ask about a second

room, and by the surprised look on Darren's face, it hadn't occurred to him either.

"We're fine," he heard himself say. Sure, it was unconventional, but sharing the space was forcing them to get along. Maybe the producers should have ordered them to be roommates years ago.

"Suit yourself. Congrats on the show. I watched it last night, and you were phenomenal, Crosby. Really, it turned out so well."

"Thanks. Jay was awesome, too," he said.

"Wasn't he?" Deb was a proud mama, he could tell, but not the kind who pushed it down your throat. "And what about you, Darren? I know you were in town while they were filming in the fall, but Jay said if I want to know what happens, I have to watch the show."

Darren laughed. "No spoilers, then. You'll have to keep watching."

"Fine, I guess I will. I'm glad you're staying another night. The roads are a mess out there. You be safe, you hear?"

"Yes, Deb," Darren said dutifully.

Crosby nodded his assent. It felt good to have someone worrying about them.

Before she left, she glanced between them, just as Max had a few minutes earlier. "It's nice to see you boys getting along," she said.

Crosby shifted, feeling suddenly warm. He had a sneaking feeling everyone was making assumptions about them.

"Yes, Crosby has been on his very best behavior," Darren said solemnly.

Crosby huffed lightly and elbowed Darren in the side. "It's been a trial, but I've been bearing up."

Deb laughed. "Glad to hear it. You let me know if you need anything, all right?"

They promised they would, and she shuffled off to keep the inn running like the well-oiled machine it was.

"She is an amazing woman," Darren declared as they made for the back exit that led to the inn's grounds and a path into the acreage of woods that separated the inn from the highway.

"Do you think she thought we—" Crosby shook his head at himself. Did it matter what she thought? He glanced at Darren. It might matter to him.

"We what?" Darren said curiously.

They pushed open the door to the outside world and were hit with the stinging cold air of the afternoon. Crosby felt exposed in more ways than one. "Never mind."

The snow had stopped falling a little while ago, and the skies were a cozy gray, making the world feel small, as if they were inside their own private snow globe. Someone had shoveled the sidewalk as far as the path, but there was at least a foot of fresh snow on the ground everywhere else. Crosby's boots were good for it, and Darren had a similar pair. They set off on the path, snow crunching softly beneath their feet. Darren leaned down and swiped a handful of snow in his borrowed mittens. He frowned down at his hands.

"It's not really packing. Too loose."

"Maybe the snow in the woods is wetter," Crosby suggested.

He tromped on. The air stung his cheeks, and he adjusted his scarf so it covered his chin and mouth. He pulled his beanie down over his forehead. He didn't see it coming until it was too late. The snowball slammed into his shoulder, exploding, and flinging wet snow onto his face. He turned and glared at Darren, who was chortling and already forming another snowball.

"Just kidding. It's perfect snowball snow."

"You fucker," Crosby said, wiping slush off his nose.

He took off for the trees, intent on making his own arsenal. He took two more direct hits before he was able to scoop a decent handful of snow. He turned around and flung it with perfect accuracy right into Darren's laughing face. The laughter abruptly stopped as Darren sputtered.

His eyes blinking away slush, Darren laughed again, ruefully this time. "I deserved that," he admitted. "Truce?"

Crosby considered. "Or we could each take five minutes to make a stockpile and then go wild."

"Better idea. On your mark, get set, go!"


Crosby was wet, cold, and winded by the time they stopped trying to smother each other with snow. The snowball fight had quickly devolved into trying to see who could shove more snow down the other's collar. He was heavier, but Darren was wriggly and wily.

Crosby flopped backwards onto the snowy ground, his body warm under its layers from the physical exertion, even as he couldn't feel the tip of his nose.

"You play dirty, Crosby," Darren panted next to him. The other man pushed himself upright, looking down at Crosby. He had lost his beanie somewhere, and his dark hair was going every which way. His gray eyes matched the sky behind him.

Crosby glanced at Darren's mouth, then away, closing his eyes against the temptation. Okay, he and Darren were co-existing. Having fun, even. It might have been too soon to tell whether or not he was getting over his crush, though. Darren had been a feature of Crosby's fantasy life for such a long time. It would take a while to retrain his brain not to think of him as an object of desire.

Crushing on him was harmless when they never interacted. Now it had the potential to mess up their tentative ceasefire.

"What are you thinking about?" Darren asked.

"Huh?"

"You have a little groove between your eyebrows." He raised his gloved hand and waved it in front of Crosby's face but didn't touch him. "What Jay and Cami call the groove of despair. Something wrong?"

"No, actually. Everything's...good."

"Well, that was convincing," Darren said. "Come on, you can tell me. What's on your mind?"

Crosby couldn't very well tell him he'd been thinking about his pathetic fifteen-year crush. "Um. I have an audition coming up in a week I'm a little nervous about."

"Oh, yeah? What's the part?"

"It's an indie movie. *Dessert First*. A romance."

"Oh, I know that project. My friend Darla is doing the costumes. She says it's going to be good."

"Oh." Crosby swallowed, sorry he'd swerved in this particular direction. "Cool."

"What part are you reading for?"

Crosby pushed himself up on his elbows and squinted at Darren. "Are you cold? Should we go in?"

"What? Why don't you want to tell me?" Darren frowned.

Crosby blustered. "It's not that." He thought for a second. "Okay, maybe a little. If you haven't figured this out by now, I'm not the most comfortable talking about myself."

"But we're friends now," Darren said eagerly. "Right?"

"One game of 'Truth or Dare,' and now we're friends?" Crosby said skeptically, though that's exactly what he'd sensed was happening. He wanted to take back the words as soon as he said them, but Darren didn't snipe back as expected.

He smiled. "Don't forget Battleship. And the snow-ball fight. Quality bonding, man."

"Yeah, I feel much closer to you after getting snow crammed down my shirt."

Darren grinned. "Me too, Crosby. Hey, does anyone

call you Spencer? Calling you Crosby makes me feel like I'm scolding you all the time."

"Pretty much only my parents," Crosby said, "which is why Spencer feels like the name I get called when I'm in trouble, not the other way around."

"Okay, never mind," Darren laughed.

"You could try it, though, if you want." What? Where did that come from?

"Maybe I will."

Crosby sat all the way up. His pants were damp from sitting in the snow. "So, should we go in and dry off?"

"You are unbelievable," Darren said. He pushed Crosby's shoulder and almost sent him sprawling back into the snow again.

"What? What did I do?"

"You are the master of deflection. Tell me what part you're reading for in *Dessert First*."

"Oh. Grady, the dessert chef," Crosby said as casually as he could.

"The lead?"

"One of them," Crosby hedged.

Darren sighed. "Look, *Spencer*," he said pointedly. Crosby winced. "Can you pretend I'm someone you can talk to about stuff? I'm on your team here, dude. We're on the same cast. We have the same friends. We live in the same city. I'm not your enemy. And I'm sure you have plenty of queer friends, but I've also been around the block a few times. So use me as a resource, okay? We've already established it's who you know in this business.

Don't make this harder than it is. It's okay to ask for help."

"What are you saying?"

"You can tell me you're trying out for a gay part. It's okay, Crosby. Spencer. Crosby. Damn. I better stick with Crosby—you already have too many names."

Crosby froze. Why did it feel like every time he shared something of himself with Darren, the other man used it as a chance to peel back another layer of his defenses? This was why it was better to keep everything safely locked inside in the first place.

But he forced himself to listen to what Darren was offering. Last night, when he'd told him he was gay, Darren had seemed genuinely regretful about the lost opportunity of being able to come up together as two out actors. He should learn from that and let him in.

It just felt like the most dangerous thing he could do to allow Darren even closer. Because Crosby wasn't going to want to stop there. He'd want more than Darren could give him, and they'd be back where they started, unable to be in the same room together.

He got up and walked back to the inn.

# Chapter Six



The Misty Harbor Inn's cozy restaurant included a bar tucked away in the corner, with views of the woods. Darren was wet and cold, but he couldn't fathom going to the room to be brushed off by Crosby for the dozenth time in two days. A drink would warm him from the inside. Maybe he'd even get dinner there and give Crosby more time to get the stick out of his ass. Presuming it hadn't been in there so long, it wasn't a permanent feature.

Only trouble was when Darren made his way to the bar, Crosby was already there. He sat on a center stool, his golden curls lit up by the overhead lamps, a frown on his face. A discontented angel.

Darren sighed, considered going back to the room, but he wanted a drink more than privacy. Besides, they had to spend another night together; he might as well try to smooth things over.

"I swear I'm not following you," Darren said as he took the empty stool next to Crosby. "But I require alcohol."

"I'll go," Crosby said immediately, shifting off his stool.

Darren suppressed a hint of anger. Was Crosby still pretending they were nothing more than indifferent co-workers?

"Come on, have a drink with me," he said, signaling to the bartender, who didn't seem to notice him as she poured a pint for another customer at the other end of the bar.

"Why do you want to have a drink with me?" Crosby said. The stiffness in his voice was classic Crosby—a veneer of asshole to cover up his uncomfortable shyness.

"Because I'm a glutton for punishment," Darren said, trying for lightness.

Crosby stared at him for a second, and then sat back down. "You're too easy on me, actually."

"What do you mean?"

He paused, seeming to gather his thoughts. "I'm difficult. I'm closed off. You won't give up on me, and it's fucking annoying. You should hate me. The fact that you haven't told me off, like, three times today, has me worried about your mental state."

Darren took a calming breath. "Look. Maybe I am trying too hard. Maybe I'm overcompensating. But I can't stop thinking about how we could have been friends all this time, and I'm more pissed at missing out on that than I am at you, so can you please meet me halfway? Please?"

Crosby didn't say anything for one beat. Then two. Darren was beginning to think the bartender was staying away on purpose, because she didn't come over to break the awkward silence either. Then finally, when Darren was about to give up on them both, Crosby started talking.

"I've never played a gay character before. And the script for *Dessert First* is really good. It could change my career. So I'm nervous. But excited. And I'm not good at talking about my auditions—it doesn't usually help my anxiety."

Darren let out an internal sigh of relief that Crosby was doing what he'd asked. He was trying, and Darren wasn't going to spook him by calling attention to it. "What does help with your anxiety?"

"Preparation. I have to know the script forward and backward. Then I go in and leave everything at the door except the part."

Preparation—something the two of them had in common. Darren also tended to deal with his newbie director nerves by over-preparing. He latched onto the practical solution, a tangible way he could help Crosby.

"I can help you prepare. We can run lines together."

"You'd want to?"

"Sure—what else are we going to do all night?" Darren felt the implications of that statement blossom in the empty space between them, but he refused to blush. He wasn't flirting with Spencer Crosby—that would be ridiculous.

"What, sick of Battleship already?" Crosby asked with a half-smile.

Just like that, they were back to their new normal—teasing without the bite. "Hey, I'm always up for a game of Battleship."

As if sensing the change in mood herself, the bartender finally came over and took Darren's order for a Glenfiddich. Crosby ordered a beer and asked for a menu.

"Can I buy you dinner?" Crosby asked, his voice soft.

"What for?"

"You put me up. I'll cover the hotel bill, too."

"We'll split it," Darren said firmly. "I'd take a simple 'thank you' anyway."

Crosby swiveled his stool to face him and said, "Thank you, Darren," with perfectly delivered sincerity.

Having the full force of Spencer Crosby's legendary green eyes on him, intense and serious, made something strange happen to Darren's stomach. He felt it sort of—flutter? It was a sensation he normally associated with nerves, showing up on the first day of a new set, a new show, hoping all of his research and meetings and prep would pay off. But right now, he wasn't nervous. He couldn't be. It was just him and Crosby and another frosty winter night at the inn stretching out in front of them.

"You're welcome," he said, when he realized Crosby was waiting for his response.

Crosby blinked, and the spell woven by those verdant eyes was broken. They ordered steaks and potatoes—baked for Darren, mashed for Crosby—and moved from the bar to a table by the window when the food was ready.

"You have the script for *Dessert First*?" Darren asked when they'd made sizable dents in their meals. Their snow fight had worked up his appetite.

"Yeah, on my computer," Crosby said. "You really wouldn't mind?"

"You know, Sawyer and Noah never get any scenes together, except the occasional group scene. I always wanted to know what it would be like to work with you," Darren said, surprising himself with the sentiment. It was true. He would page through every script, hoping for a scene with Crosby, if only because the blond would be forced to acknowledge his existence.

"You're right," he said. "Maybe there'll be a chance in the second season of the new show."

"You'd want that?" Darren asked, curiously.

"I—" Crosby looked like he was about to say one thing and changed his mind. "Yeah," he said eventually. "And I hope you get to direct, too."

"From your lips to the producers' ears."

Crosby hummed. "What else are you up for?"

"I'm about to do an episode of a network hospital show. We did locations last week, but shooting isn't until mid-January. One of the locations is right around the corner from my apartment, which is surreal. Sometimes it feels like all of New York is one big backlot."

"Where?"

"Chelsea," he said. "I'm on Twenty-fourth between Ninth and Tenth."

Crosby's jaw went slack. "I'm on Twenty-second and Ninth."

"We live in the same neighborhood. Small world." Darren wondered why he'd never run into Crosby on the street—had the dark thought maybe Crosby would go out of his way to avoid him if he did see him. He wasn't convinced Crosby's shyness and sexual identity crisis were the entire explanation for the uncomfortable energy between them all this time.

But Crosby was right about one thing—maybe Darren cared too much about getting people to like him. Maybe he should let this go.

*Fresh start, remember?*

"I only moved there a few months ago," Crosby said, "from Harlem. I got sick of the subway always getting shut down."

"That explains it," Darren said. "It's a great neighborhood. I've been there for years. Have you tried The Pho 2? Best pho in the city."

"I will now," Crosby said, and he smiled. Darren got

that funny flutter in his belly again. What was going on with him?

They debated ordering dessert, but Crosby reminded him they still had a few pastries from Misty Harbor Bakeshop in their room.

"We'll have to jog back to Manhattan to work off the calories," Darren said, patting his stomach.

Crosby smirked. "Digging out our cars will probably suffice."

Darren groaned. "Aren't we getting a warm spell? Maybe we won't have to dig."

"I think it's supposed to snow more the day after tomorrow. If we want to get out of here, tomorrow is the day."

"Oh." Of course, they had to think about getting back to the city. "I hope the hotel has some kind of digging implement we can borrow. Like a trowel?"

"You are such a city boy, aren't you?" Crosby said.

"What, and you aren't?"

"I spent four months shooting a miniseries in Alaska. I learned how to do winter."

"*Yukon Dreams*, right?" Darren said. "With Chris Capshaw."

"Yeah."

"I dated Chris for a while—he's a good guy," he said offhandedly.

Crosby said nothing.

"What? You didn't like him either?" Darren tried not to seem accusatory.

"What do you mean 'either?'"

Darren shrugged. "Never mind."

Crosby took a deep breath. "He was good to work with."

"Surprised he didn't make a pass at you," Darren said. Chris was nice, but he was a terrible flirt, and if he'd sensed an opening with Spencer Crosby, he would have rushed through in a heartbeat.

"I've never—" Crosby stopped, and for a long moment Darren hung in suspense, wondering how he was going to finish that sentence. "—dated a co-star."

Darren relaxed. "Oh. Why not?"

Crosby licked his lips. He had really nice lips. Had Darren ever noticed before? Of course he'd noticed, in the way you couldn't deny a fact like the sky was blue or ice cream was delicious. But he'd never fixated on Crosby's lips before, and now he couldn't seem to stop his gaze from drifting toward them, struck anew each time by how almost offensively pretty they were.

"Why do you think?" Crosby said, and Darren had to remind himself what they were talking about. Oh right, dating co-stars.

"Because you're smart," Darren said, pulling his gaze to Crosby's eyes. They weren't any less distracting than his lips, with their clear, almost otherworldly green. Damn. Darren needed to get his shit together.

Crosby huffed. "I thought you were going to say socially awkward."

"That, too. But it's smart to avoid potential drama. Believe me, I've been in a few sketchy situations in my day. Better to keep your work life and personal life separate."

For some reason, this made Crosby's groove of despair come back. "What about Jay and Cami?"

"They're freaks. Soulmates or some shit," Darren said. "And they had their fair share of drama behind the scenes, too, don't you remember?"

"Yeah, I suppose you're right." Crosby fiddled with his water glass. "So, have you ever dated a co-star?"

Darren stretched his mouth into a wicked smile. "Dated might be a stretch, but yeah. Sure. Of course."

"What about as a director?" Crosby asked.

"No," Darren said quickly. "That would be a terrible idea. No way."

"Potentially messy," Crosby agreed.

"Directing is enough to manage without throwing a fling into the mix."

"So is that all you do? Flings?" Crosby sounded curious, not judgmental.

Darren pushed the last of his food around his plate. "No. Not always." Lately, especially, as he'd been watching his friends pair off, he could see the writing on the wall. The single lifestyle had started getting stale the minute he hit his thirties. How much less appealing would it be in another decade?

"I've had a few long-term relationships. Nothing's stuck yet. But someday. I want something that'll last, with someone who wants a kid. I don't want to be an ancient dad. I'll do it on my own if I have to, but parenting with a partner seems way easier."

He glanced up, and Crosby was watching him. There was an undefinable expression on his face. No, wait, Darren could put a name to it—Crosby looked stunned.

"What, you thought I was a slut or something?" Darren had gone through his slutty phase—don't get him wrong. He hadn't found Mr. Right yet, but that didn't mean it wasn't fun looking. But it had been a while since he'd hooked up just for the hell of it.

"No, not exactly. I can't believe you're so comfortable sharing stuff like that. I'm not even that open with my therapist," Crosby said.

"Sorry, TMI, I guess." Darren didn't know what the big deal was. You had feelings, you shared them, or not, and the world kept on spinning.

"Don't apologize. I wish I could come out and say stuff. I have to have known someone for like—"

"Fifteen years?" Darren broke in dryly. "Crosby, we're hardly strangers."

"Point," Crosby acknowledged, with a tip of his head. "I was raised by people who save showing their feelings for when the script calls for it. I'm jealous of you. Again."

Darren felt another stab of sympathy for the guy. "You know what? I think you can be open in small groups. Look at us, just two guys hanging out and talking like regular people. On a set like *Sawyer's Cove*, there are so many people around. Maybe that's why we never connected. Too much of a group experience. What do you think?"

Crosby pressed his lips together, considering. "I am usually better in small groups, it's true." He rubbed the pads of his thick, elegant fingers over his unreal lips. Darren was mesmerized by the motion. "But there's another reason we never got to be friends."

"Oh, yeah?" Darren leaned forward eagerly. He'd suspected there was something else going on.

"I had this massive—" Crosby abruptly cut off, his face glowing the same shade as a red bulb on a string of Christmas lights.

Darren goggled. "You cannot leave me an opening like that, man. Massive what? Ego? I wanna say 'dick' so bad, but I'm a grown-up. Okay, I guess I said it anyway."

Crosby cracked a brief, anguished smile, then said three words Darren never expected to hear from his beautiful mouth. "Crush. On you."

# Chapter Seven



Crosby couldn't believe he'd come out and said it. He'd kept his crush on Darren Silverstein a secret for years, not even telling Ariel about it, and Ariel had a way of winkling everything out of a person.

He'd longed to be like Darren for a brief moment—someone who said what he felt, said what he thought. Someone who shared details of his own life as if it was as easy as ordering a steak. Darren had shared something with him. He wanted a partner, and a kid. Crosby had wanted to honor that with a confidence of his own.

But he was pretty sure he'd miscalculated when

Darren said nothing in response to his blurted-out confession. Darren opened and closed his mouth a few times, his gray eyes wide.

He was about to backtrack or laugh it off, or maybe go throw himself into a snowbank. He'd heard hypothermia wasn't the worst way to die. But before he could commit to an action, his phone buzzed with a text. He seized on the distraction, thumbing at the screen frantically.

TREVOR

I'm at the inn. Want to make snow angels?

Crosby looked up, and Darren was still staring at him as if he'd acquired full clown makeup at some point since they sat down to dinner.

"Um. Trevor wants to hang out. I think I should go."

"The massive thing you had was a *crush* on me?" Darren said, ignoring Crosby's feeble attempt at escape.

Crosby mustered all of the haughtiness he'd perfected over the years. "Sorry, just trying to be more open," he said in his chilliest tone, then started typing out a text.

I'm in the restaurant. Meet y

Darren spoke in a voice so loud Crosby jumped, and his finger slipped, causing him to send the unfinished text.

*Damn.*

"You're telling me you made me feel like shit for three years because you *liked me?*"

"No!" That made Crosby seem like he'd hurt Darren intentionally. He glanced around the room, but no one was paying them attention. Still, he lowered his voice and leaned across the table. "I already told you I was confused, and everyone is stupid when they're eighteen. Right?"

Darren crossed his arms, grabbing each of his shoulders with the opposite hand. "Wow. I mean, really, wow. Sorry. That's so not what I was expecting you to say."

Crosby's attempt at being free and open had backfired spectacularly. Not only did Darren seem thrown, the easiness between them had vanished. Instead of feeling lighter, as if the truth would help him move on from his feelings, he wished he could call the words back and fit himself back into his glass case of superiority. But all his defense mechanisms were inadequate in the face of sharing his secret with the one person who never should have found out.

He forced out a laugh that sounded like a cat being strangled. "Well, surprise."

"Surprise!" A new voice, but a familiar one. Trevor strode up to their table in a puffy black jacket, hot pink scarf, and rainbow knit cap over his shoulder-length straight blond hair.

"Hey!" Crosby pushed back from the table so quickly the flatware rattled. "What's up?"

"There are only so many times I can watch *American Werewolf in London* without wanting to write David/Jack fanfiction. Besides, my road finally got plowed, so I figured I should escape before the next batch of snow gets here." He looked at Darren and flashed what Crosby thought of as his "customer service" smile. "Hi, I'm Trevor."

"Hi. I'm Darren."

"I know." Trevor's impersonal smile dropped. "You probably get this all the time, but Noah is such an important character. Thank you."

Crosby lifted his eyebrows. Trevor was usually much more effusive. But maybe some things were too important to go overboard with.

Darren did probably hear it all the time, but he nodded easily. "Thanks for saying that. And thanks for the amazing pastries—what a fantastic care package."

Trevor's rouged cheeks turned even pinker. "You're welcome." He glanced at Crosby. "Well, aren't we all so polite? What are you handsome men up to? Did you use the gloves I gave you? Should we go build a snowman?"

"It's dark," Crosby said while Darren put in, "We did have a snowball fight."

"Oh, boo, I miss all the fun." Trevor pouted. "Let's do something. I'm so bored. The shop's closed until after New Year's so Zelda can take a proper vacation, and Lord knows that woman needs it, but I need a distraction."

"We have been playing games," Darren said. "Like 'Truth or Dare.'" He said "truth" pointedly, as if Crosby had been lying all this time.

"Fun! What about 'Two Truths and a Lie?' Classic icebreaker."

Crosby was about to beg Trevor to take him back to his mother's house. He'd rather watch *An American Were-wolf in London* on repeat than have to face Darren with his secret no longer safely under lock and key.

"I'm game," Darren said. "Do you want a drink?"

"I'll get a tea. You boys want another round?" Trevor asked.

Darren nodded while Crosby shook his head no. Alcohol wasn't going to help this clusterfuck get un-clustered.

To Crosby, Trevor said, "Get me a chair?" before he went to the bar to order.

Crosby gulped. What was happening right now? Trevor was supposed to be his escape route, and now they were all going to play some stupid game?

"Come on, sit down, Crosby," Darren said sharply. "You owe me."

"Excuse me?"

Darren was being...un-Darren-like. He was twitchy and prickly. Crosby was reminded of a fish who seemed harmless but all of a sudden blew up to twice its size and revealed sharp spines all over its body.

Apparently done waiting for Crosby to get his bear-ings, Darren got up and dragged an extra chair over to their small table. He flopped back down in his seat.

"You love games," Darren said acidly. "Let's play."

"Maybe I don't want to play," Crosby said, his natural defenses falling into their well-worn groves.

"What? You love games," Trevor said, appearing at the table and plopping into the chair between them, holding a steaming mug in one hand and depositing another whisky in front of Darren. "I'll go first."

Crosby admitted defeat. He sank into his own chair slowly. "Fine."

"Fine, Grumpy Gus. What's gotten into him?" Trevor asked Darren conspiratorially, as if they were now best friends united against him. Great. Just what he needed—for Darren to steal the only friend he had in Misty Harbor.

He crossed his arms over his chest and stuck his chin out.

"He's experimenting with being free," Darren said.

"Huh. Okay. Interesting. Two truths and a lie." Trevor set his mug on the table and began counting them on his slender fingers. "One, I've never seen *Titanic*. Two, my favorite vegetable is asparagus. Three, I once had an imaginary friend named Jillian."

Darren smiled. "Easy. The lie has gotta be the asparagus. Who likes those wilted little sticks?"

"What's your vote?" Trevor asked, shifting toward Crosby.

"*Titanic*," Crosby barked out. "There's no way you haven't seen it."

Trevor made a surprisingly accurate buzzer noise. "Got both of you. I have never seen *Titanic*. You know my stance on movie length, Crosby. All movies should be no more than an hour and forty minutes." He twisted to look at Darren. "By the way, asparagus is delicious. You've clearly never had Zelda's asparagus vinaigrette. Heathen."

"So you didn't have an imaginary friend?" Darren asked skeptically.

"Oh, I had an imaginary friend," Trevor said, "But her name wasn't Jillian. That's the secret to this game, fellas, keep the lie as close to the truth as possible, and it throws everyone off."

Darren laughed. "Devious. You'd make a good actor."

Trevor took a sip of his tea and pursed his lips in a pleased smile. "Thanks. I'm actually taking an acting class."

"You are?" Crosby said as Darren commented, "Cool."

"Yeah." Trevor shrugged with what Crosby suspected was forced nonchalance. "I've been thinking about it for a while, and Cami told me about this online acting studio her friend runs. It's challenging but fun. I'd have to go to New York or Boston to take in person classes, but this is good for now."

"I had no idea you were interested in acting," Crosby said, feeling a little hurt Trevor hadn't told him about this before.

"Well, you can only rub shoulders with famous actors for so long before you get the bug." Trevor smiled, but again, Crosby got the sense he was putting on a casual front. Since he'd played that game himself, he decided to let Trevor off the hook. For now.

"So what was your imaginary friend's name?" Crosby said, changing the subject back to the game.

"Bob," Trevor said succinctly.

Darren laughed, and Crosby joined him.

"Okay, weirdo," Darren said, with affection in his voice. "Who's next?"

"You go, Crosby," Trevor said, nudging his foot under the table.

Crosby's mind raced. He should have been thinking about this long before now if he wanted to win. He considered what to say. Innocuous? Or should he throw them off with something obscure? In the end, he went with the first things that came to mind.

"I'm allergic to pineapple. I've never been to Disneyland. And I'm afraid of parrots."

Trevor burst out laughing. "Please tell me the lie is the parrot thing. Who's afraid of parrots?"

"Gotta be Disneyland. You seem like a closet Disney freak," Darren said, some of his normal good humor returning.

"Another point for Trevor. I am not afraid of parrots. But I don't like them. They're unsettlingly intelligent."

"You've never been to Disneyland? How is this possible? And we must rectify the oversight immediately." Darren looked like he was about to yank out his phone to book a flight to California right then and there.

"I've been to Disney World. About a dozen times," Crosby confessed. He didn't want Darren to think he was a complete troglodyte. "But never Disneyland."

"Jesus, you scared me," Darren said, putting a hand to his chest like a Tennessee Williams heroine. "But if you're allergic to pineapple, that means—"

"No Dole whip at Disney," Crosby finished. "I know. Tragic, right?"

"Okay, clearly your life is very sad, therefore you're forgiven for—" Darren cut himself off and glanced at Trevor. Surely, he wasn't going to mention his crush?

Darren seemed to reconsider whatever he was about to say. "Well, you're forgiven."

"Didn't know there was anything to forgive," Crosby muttered. Darren was acting like he'd admitted to kicking puppies instead of a harmless, unrequited crush.

Trevor glanced between the two of them, practically quivering with curiosity over the undercurrents of potential gossip, but he restrained himself. "Your turn, Darren."

"So far, Trevor is killing it. Let me think." He folded his arms over his chest, and Crosby noticed the way his long fingers wrapped around his elbows. "Okay, let's do this. I'm going to say three things about myself. Two of them will be true. One of them will be a lie. Will you be able to guess the—"

"Stop stalling," Trevor ordered.

"Fine." Darren sat forward, adopted a solemn tone. "I have a tattoo of a butterfly. I once won a roller-skating championship. And my favorite color is green."

"Where is this alleged tattoo?" Trevor asked.

"No follow-up questions allowed. That wasn't stated at the outset of the game."

"Fine. Stickler." Trevor stuck his tongue out and said, "I vote for the roller-skating championship. Sounds fake."

Crosby tried to imagine Darren with any tattoo at all. He'd never noticed one. But the favorite color thing was too innocuous to be a red herring. "Favorite color," he decided.

"Woo hoo, one point for me! I can't believe you guys think I have a butterfly tattoo."

"I need the story of the roller skating thing," Trevor said.

Darren leaned back and told them a long, intermittently hilarious story of being a fourteen-year-old trying to impress an older boy who worked at the local skating rink. Crosby only half-listened to the tale, instead letting himself relax and just watch Darren. With Trevor there, the painful sensation of being in the crosshairs of Darren's laser focus was lessened. Despite having revealed his stupid crush, even if Darren's initial reaction had stung, he'd survived. They were still talking to each other. Could maybe still be friends.

Problem was, he was no longer a confused teenager with his first crush on a boy. He was a grown man, and the object of his crush had grown up, too. Into Darren. Who was smart, funny, clever, and more handsome now than he'd been as a gangly teenager, and Crosby had always thought he was pretty fucking handsome.

Now they were no longer so wary around each other, Crosby was learning things about Darren that only made him more attractive. He wanted a partner. He wanted a kid. Crosby had assumed kids weren't going to be in the picture for him, but that didn't mean the vision of a little dark-haired, gray-eyed boy or girl looking up at Darren with love in their eyes wasn't stupidly appealing.

The thing was, Crosby came off as stuffy and arrogant because he was shy and had never been comfortable being himself, except around a very few people, and only when he was one-on-one with them. He also overthought everything, from his clothes to his acting choices. Darren would never understand being in a crowd of people and being absolutely frozen with not knowing what to do, even when most of those people in the crowd were people he knew and liked.

Crosby was also a romantic. He believed in the kind of love portrayed on TV shows like *Sawyer's Cove*—the kind of love that made people do idiotic things, that ruined lives and broke hearts. But he'd been way too shy, insecure, and scared to go after any relationship where that kind of love could be a possibility. He'd pined over Darren himself for three years without saying a word instead of finding a person he could actually work up the nerve to date.

He was a fool and a coward and being around someone like Darren, who was neither, was only putting his own sad life choices into relief. He liked his life. He was proud of his career. He liked his tidy apartment and gleaming sports car. He liked his friends. He even liked the guys he dated: safe, boring guys who had no idea what his life was really like. But he'd never been in love. Not the kind of all-consuming love he'd been led to believe had made his mother quit her career so she could share her life with his father. Instead of turning bitter or bored, she was content, and they were as in love as ever over thirty years later. They loved each other so much, sometimes he felt like an afterthought—if he ever had a child, he hoped he'd love the other parent, but he knew he'd never make the child feel second best.

"And then I found out the prize was a year's free pass to the rink," Darren said, apparently the capstone on his story. Trevor was laughing so hard, tears leaked from the corners of his eyes. Crosby chuckled, pretending he'd been paying attention.

"As much as I'd like to keep getting to know weird facts about you, Darren, I better get home before the sidewalks freeze solid." Trevor stood up, "Walk me to the lobby, Crosby?"

"Sure." He glanced at Darren, who stood up, too, and waved to Trevor.

"Nice to meet you. I'm sure I'll be seeing you."

"I hope so." Trevor smiled at him sunnily.

"See you back at the room?" Darren asked.

Darren was acting as if Crosby might not come back. It wasn't like he had much of a choice, given all his stuff was there. He simply nodded. Darren caught his gaze and lifted his chin in answer. It seemed he wasn't holding Crosby's little confession against him. Crosby reminded himself this time tomorrow he'd be back in his apartment, and Darren would once again be simply another work acquaintance.

He tried not to feel despondent. He hadn't wanted this enforced closeness in the first place, but now that he knew what it felt like to interact with Darren, he didn't look forward to giving it up.

Trevor led him to the elevators and tapped the call button. "So, that was interesting."

"Another name to cross off your *Sawyer's Cove* bingo card," Crosby said.

"You don't mind me coming by, do you?" Trevor sounded suddenly anxious. "I really wanted to check on you. I don't want you to think I used you to meet my adolescent crush."

Crosby choked on his own tongue, recovered as they walked into the waiting elevator. "The thought never crossed my mind. You had a crush on Darren?"

"On Noah more than Darren," Trevor mused. "He was so cute and so twinky compared to Will. More attainable, for sure. What about you?" Trevor side-eyed him, and Crosby cringed. He had a way of seeing everything you didn't want him to see. "Can you honestly tell me you weren't into him?"

"So, you're taking an acting class—that's really awesome. I could find out about acting classes in New York if you want."

"That is a very nice offer, and I might take you up on it, but you're not getting away with such a blatant subject change."

Crosby sighed and put a hand over his face. "I wasn't into Noah. But Darren—yeah. I told him about it right before you showed up."

Trevor gasped as the elevator let them out in the lobby. He dragged Crosby to an empty corner of the open space. "Seriously? Is that the weird vibe I was picking up? You told him you have a crush on him?"

"*Had*. Had a crush on him," Crosby said. All that was in the past. Wasn't it?

"Whatever. The guy is still gorgeous. And you two are spending the night together in a hotel room. This could not be more perfect. You have to go for it."

Crosby sputtered.

"You like him, he likes you, you're two consenting adults. What else are you going to do all night?"

There it was again, the implication that he and Darren needed something to fill the hours until dawn. They could simply go to sleep, like they did last night. Nothing had to change. He didn't have to do anything about the way he was feeling. Telling Darren he liked him once upon a time was mortifying enough. What if he made a pass and Darren was offended? Or laughed at him? They still had to work with each other on the next two seasons of *Sawyer's Cove*. There were reasons he'd never slept with a co-star, and all of those reasons were still valid.

Besides, he wasn't looking for a one-night stand. Not with the guy he'd wanted for so long. Darren wasn't the kind of guy he'd be able to get out of his system with a onetime fuck. No way.

"All I'm saying is, you only live once. Blame it on the snowstorm," Trevor advised blithely. "Speaking of which, be careful on the road tomorrow. Make sure you get out before the snow starts up again."

"I will." Crosby said mechanically. "Be safe."

"You need any condoms?" Trevor asked at full volume. "I happen to know they keep some at the front desk."

"I do not need any condoms," Crosby hissed,

glancing around the lobby. It was mostly empty, but you never knew who had a cell phone ready to record. "Now get out of here before you get me in trouble."

Trevor left with an irritatingly knowing wave. Crosby avoided making eye contact with Max's nighttime replacement at the front desk. He did not need condoms because he was not going to have sex with anybody, least of all Darren.

Besides, he had his own stash.

# Chapter Eight



Darren flagged down their server after Trevor and Crosby left and charged the dinner bill to the room, planning to take care of the whole thing without bothering Crosby. He couldn't quibble about money when his entire world was shifting on its axis. Okay, maybe he was being a little dramatic, but that's what it felt like. All those brooding, grouchy looks, all the times Crosby had avoided being alone with him or had ducked out of cast parties early. It wasn't because he hated

Darren. It was because Crosby was a closeted teenager with a crush on him.

He thought back to those early days on set. He'd been brought in midway through the first season as a guest star to play Noah, a possible love interest for Will, who was played by Nash Speedwell. He'd already done a few guest roles on New York-based shows, procedurals, murder-of-the-week type stuff, playing troubled or endangered teens. *Sawyer's Cove* was different, a show for teenagers, not adults, and the writing was sharp and fresh.

Even though the core five actors had already bonded by the time he showed up, they were welcoming to him. He'd been most worried about Nash, a straight guy playing a gay kid, afraid he might overcompensate by making Darren feel awkward during the scenes where they had to flirt and eventually be physical together. But Nash had been chill, had welcomed Darren's feedback on some of his acting choices; they'd become really good friends over the subsequent seasons.

Noah wasn't in every episode, not by a long shot, but he and Will ended up staying together for the whole run, and the role had led to a lot of other guest parts. Darren had never landed the lead role in a show of his own, though he'd been in a few pilots. He'd always been quietly relieved when they never got picked up. He never wanted the pressure of heading an entire show.

Instead, he'd turned to directing, which he found much more challenging and interesting. Unfortunately, the work was hardly steady. He still went out for acting jobs, because that's how he paid the bills. Working in the entertainment industry was never a sure thing, and mild panic set in every time he realized he didn't have his next gig lined up yet.

But those early days of *Sawyer's Cove*, man, those were fun. Joking around with Nash, Jay and Cami transparently into each other, Ariel the unofficial mama bear of the group. Even Crosby could be fun on set when he wanted to be.

Darren pictured seventeen-year-old Spencer Crosby and thought about how he'd react if he knew Crosby liked him. He would probably have pinched himself and fucking gone for it. Crosby was smoking hot back then, lithe body poured into white T-shirts and skinny jeans, cheekbones for days. Darren knew he was a reasonably good-looking guy, but he wasn't a Renaissance painting brought to life, for fuck's sake. Anyone in their right mind would say yes to Crosby.

But Darren hadn't had a chance, because Crosby had hidden his feelings behind a layer of arrogance and snobbery. Darren was finding out literally a decade and a half later that Crosby wasn't a jerk, just an insecure teenager, not sure what to do with his attraction to his co-star. Fuck.

It made sense in retrospect, but the feeling of loss Darren had been experiencing all weekend over his and Crosby's would-be friendship was only intensified by this new revelation. They had so much ground to cover, so much to catch up on.

He had an irrepressible urge to keep Crosby up all

night, interrogating him about everything from his favorite movie to his first kiss. He wanted to know everything about him. He didn't want to leave the Misty Harbor Inn tomorrow and go back to mere acquaintances. Now that he'd broken through Crosby's shell, the guy was stuck with him.

Darren didn't examine too closely why he felt so strongly about this. The answer might be embarrassing. Or too telling.

Back in the room, he changed into his sweats. He was running out of clean clothes, but he could make it one more day. He double-checked the weather; they'd have to get up early and dig out the cars if they wanted to get back to the city before the storm passed by on its return trip.

He was beginning to wonder if Crosby had abandoned him when the door clicked open and Crosby came inside, cheeks pink.

"Hey," Darren said, more relieved than he expected to be at Crosby's return.

"Hey." Crosby hovered in the doorjamb. He seemed like he had something on his mind. Was this where he told Darren he and Trevor were hooking up? He liked the guy—he was a lot of fun, and he had a unique look. Maybe he and Crosby had a friends-with-benefits situation. The idea curdled Darren's stomach.

"You coming in or—?"

"Oh, right. Yeah." Crosby shut the door and started removing his layers. He pulled off his scarf, the color of which was the exact color of his eyes. "I hope I didn't make things weird."

"Huh?"

"I guess you have a right to be pissed," Crosby went on.

Darren seriously didn't know what Crosby was talking about. "I'm not pissed." He wouldn't be *mad* if Crosby and Trevor were hooking up—just disappointed.

"You sounded kind of pissed in the restaurant."

Darren finally realized Crosby was talking about the crush thing. "Oh. Well. I was taken aback. I never thought in a million years—"

Crosby's mouth thinned into a line. "Is it that unbelievable?"

Darren couldn't say the right thing, apparently. "I was just thinking about what I would have done if I'd known. I'd probably have jumped at the chance."

Crosby's eyes widened comically large. Darren couldn't believe how fucking *green* they were.

"Really?" Crosby's voice was strangely high-pitched, and he cleared his throat and said, "I mean, really?" in a more normal register.

"We'll never know, right?" Darren chuckled awkwardly. "It was all so long ago."

"Yeah, ancient history," Crosby agreed.

"Let's focus on right now," Darren suggested, remembering his earlier offer. "Wanna read those lines?"

"You still want to?"

"Sure, why not? I heard the script is pretty good."

"It's charming," Crosby said, and Darren smiled.

Only Spencer Crosby could call a script for a gay rom com charming and not sound pretentious. All right, he did sound pretentious, but in a genuine way.

Crosby was pretty charming himself, Darren could admit. His stiff shyness was kind of endearing once you realized he wasn't privately considering you an idiot.

"Yeah, get the script out," Darren said, jumping onto his bed. "Do you know what scenes you're doing at the audition?"

"They told me what to prepare. I'm having the most trouble with this one scene, but—anyway, I can do the monologue."

"You can work on a monologue by yourself anytime," Darren said. "Pick something else. Come on, I'm a good scene partner, I promise."

Crosby got out his laptop and opened it. He looked at Darren with a hesitant expression. "I have to log in to this site to see the script. They won't let me download it."

"Darn, there go my plans to pirate it." Darren patted the bed next to him. "Sit here—that way we can both see. Are you off book?"

"Mostly." Crosby waited a beat, then sat down gingerly on the bed, balancing the computer on his lap. "Okay, I'm Grady, you're Hank."

"Hank. Got it. What's the setup?"

"We've been star crossed since the beginning, never the right place or the right time. We're at a party, and our dates end up ditching us, and we're finally, maybe, going to leave the friend zone."

"Sounds like a lot of tension. Love it," Darren said,

trying to keep it light. He hadn't exactly thought this through when he'd offered to read. He'd forgotten *Dessert First* was a romantic comedy, which implied—duh—romance. And he'd been having way too many uncomfortably romantic thoughts about Crosby in the last few hours.

But he was a professional. He deliberately kept a yard of bed between them. "Aren't scenes like this usually reserved for chemistry reads?"

"I'm hoping that's why they gave it to me. I heard they have it narrowed down to me and one other guy. So, maybe this *is* the chemistry read."

"Nice. Okay. Let's do it."

Crosby closed his eyes and took a deep breath. Darren had seen him do that often on set when he was trying to settle himself before going into a scene. When he opened his eyes again, he looked different; not exactly like Spencer Crosby, not like Sawyer North. He was different, a third person. He was Grady.

"Looks like we've both been ditched."

Darren read the next line. He wasn't trying to hit a home run, but he wanted to give Crosby something to work off. He imagined being a guy who was going to dump whatever loser he'd come to the party with and finally hook up with a guy like Grady.

"Yeah, Blake was on call. Doctors, am I right?"

"Selfish bastards," Crosby-as-Grady said.

"The absolute worst. What's your boy's excuse?"

"Joe isn't feeling well."

"Too bad."

"Yeah," Crosby scoffed. Then, sadder, "I think he's cheating on me."

"Seriously? Dude, that's fucked up."

"I know. I'm too lazy to break up with him." A fake smile.

Darren felt himself get caught up in Crosby's performance. Fuck, Crosby was a good actor. Darren felt the unspoken layers of his offhanded comment and ached for him.

"You ever cheat on him?" Darren-as-Hank said. He dropped his voice, made the question sound like an invitation.

Crosby glanced at Darren's lips. He smiled, mysterious. "Not while sober. Joe and I have a deal. It doesn't count if you're drunk."

"Dark."

"Realistic."

Darren read the next line, realizing far too late where this scene was going. He wet his lips and made eye contact with Crosby. Not Crosby. Grady. This was just acting. He'd done it a thousand times before.

"So, are you drunk?"

Crosby must have been aware of the next stage direction, but instead of going in for the kiss written in the script, he looked at the screen, frowned.

"Can we go again? I want to try something different."

Darren blinked, oddly bereft. It's not like they'd definitely make Crosby kiss whoever was reading opposite him in the audition room, but what if they asked him to? Wouldn't Mr. Prepared want to be, well, prepared?

He didn't argue. This was Crosby's study session. "Sure."

He rearranged himself on the bed, turning with one leg folded up beneath him. They were only about a foot apart now, the computer resting on the comforter between them. Crosby did his eyes-closed centering thing, and they ran through the lines. Darren barely had to glance at the script this time. He was used to picking up lines quickly and discarding them just as quickly once they had been committed to film.

On this go-round, they picked up the pace of the banter, and all too soon they were at the moment when Grady was supposed to answer Hank's question with a kiss. Again, Crosby backed off.

"What about the rest of the scene?" Darren found himself saying. "Should we keep going?"

Crosby looked at the computer screen instead of Darren. "It couldn't hurt," he said finally. "If you don't mind."

"No, this is fun. I really love directing, but sometimes it's fun to be someone else for a while, you know?"

Crosby smiled. "Yeah, I do know. I can't believe we get paid to dress up and play pretend."

"It's a racket, isn't it? Let's go again, from the beginning," Darren urged.

"Wait, um. You have any notes? Being a director and everything?" Crosby was affecting indifference, but Darren had lately become a student of Crosby's tells, and he knew Crosby wanted a serious answer.

"You're doing great," Darren said, which was true. "But—"

"But?"

"I get the sadness, the shame Grady has about his loser boyfriend, that's coming through loud and clear. I'm not sure I'm getting Grady's attraction to Hank as much, though. Aren't Grady and Hank endgame in this story? The audience will be rooting for them. But right now, I'm not sure Grady even thinks Hank is attractive."

He watched Crosby consider the feedback. "Okay, I hear that," he said evenly.

Darren was mildly surprised. He'd always thought Crosby was a little bit of a diva, but that was clearly unfair. He was open to feedback. Darren hoped he'd get a chance to direct *Sawyer's Cove,* not only because it would be a fun challenge and great for his resume, but so he could direct Crosby, for real.

"Give me a minute."

Crosby scrolled through the pages again and repositioned himself, turning so he faced Darren completely. As he scooted closer on the bed, the laptop bobbed up and down. He was only inches away now. Both of them affected the posture of two guys at the tail end of the night, tired but also a little wired, and this time when Crosby began, his attention was really on Darren—no, on *Hank.*

Darren felt the shift like a zing of electricity up his spine as he tried to keep up with Crosby's new intensity. Now it seemed as if not only was Grady into Hank—he wanted to throw down right then and there. Darren's cheeks warmed as Crosby said the line about it not being cheating if they're drunk, his voice now full of intention. He stuttered over the next line.

"D-dark."

Crosby smiled wickedly. "Realistic."

"So, are you drunk?" Darren asked, and this time, instead of pulling away, Crosby leaned in, halving the distance between them. Darren lowered his eyelids in anticipation of being kissed, but Crosby still didn't seal the deal.

Darren was fed up on behalf of poor Hank, sick of being teased by Crosby's inviting mouth. He tipped forward a few more inches until his face bumped into Crosby's. According to the script, Grady was supposed to initiate the kiss, then break it off, with lines about how he can't, that he's not drunk enough for this.

Darren forgot all about the script the moment he touched Crosby's soft lips with his own.

Crosby froze, then just as quickly relaxed. Carefully, Darren kept up the kiss, mind blank. He didn't think about the script or the characters or anything at all except kissing Crosby.

*Crosby.* He was kissing Spencer Crosby.

It was so unbelievable that, for a moment, he was certain he must be dreaming. But then Crosby's lips parted a fraction, and Darren could taste the bitterness of the IPA he'd had with his meal in the restaurant. Not a dream then.

He shivered, adjusted the angle so the kiss was no longer chaste experimentation or a type of stage kiss, but a full-on kiss between two adults, where the result might be any number of interesting outcomes. Darren wanted to dart his tongue out more than anything, but he couldn't quite bring himself to cross that line. He already felt overheated; the taste of Crosby in his mouth was going to his head. Adding tongue would turn this into making out. Making out wasn't in the script. But it felt too good to stop.

He was caught in a horrible limbo, and the only solution seemed to be to keep kissing Crosby. Maybe forever.

# Chapter Nine

---

@sawyerscovedaily Oh boy. That kiss. You know what I'm talking about. #ineedacoldshower #lilyer #sawly #sawyerscove #episode2

---

Crosby often lost himself in his characters. He liked to *be* the person in the script, to bring the words to physical life and take a break from being himself. It was one of the perks of his profession—getting a vacation from his shy, awkward self and trying on someone else's personality for size.

So when Darren, playing the part of Hank, who his character, Grady, very much wanted to kiss, kissed him, at first it made perfect sense. It even said it right there in the script—GRADY KISSES HANK. An unambiguous stage direction if there ever was one. Darren had obviously read the same words Crosby had.

But what might have begun as a stage kiss had crossed over into uncharted territory. Darren moved his head, opened his mouth, and now they were actually kissing each other. The unmistakable shift and slide of lips, the taste of Darren's after-dinner whisky, the scent of the inn's signature soap on Darren's skin.

Darren was kissing him.

And Crosby was kissing back.

He should pull away. He should wipe his mouth and make a joke about stage kissing. He should put a stop to it. Darren must have gotten carried away with the scene —he wouldn't want to be actually kissing Crosby.

*All evidence to the contrary*, Crosby's mind supplied as the pressure from Darren's lips increased and Crosby responded in kind. They were trading kisses now, no other body part touching except their mouths. They weren't even kissing with tongue, but it was still the hottest kiss Crosby had ever experienced.

Because this was Darren Silverstein.

Crosby had watched him kiss Nash Speedwell enough times to know Darren had to be a good kisser. His lips weren't overly plump, like Crosby's, but they were full enough to give his partner something to work with. Darren seemed to smile through his kisses, and this was no exception. Crosby felt the curve of his mouth against his, as if he found the encounter amusing. Or perhaps simply pleasurable.

Was that possible? Could Crosby be giving Darren pleasure? Fuck, the concept went straight to his dick; he was getting hard. His face went hot at this development, and his hands, which had been keeping him anchored to the bed under the onslaught of Darren's mouth, suddenly felt overlarge and clumsy. Should he touch Darren? Should he cover himself up? Should he stop kissing the guy he'd wanted to kiss for almost half his life?

So many options, and none of them good.

He'd pretty much resigned himself to having to spend the rest of his life on this bed, mouth fused to Darren's. At least that way they'd never have to talk about it, even if they died from dehydration and chapped lips.

Then Darren's tongue finally, *finally* breached Crosby's mouth, and it was shockingly good. His involuntary groan was so loud, he startled himself into motion, springing back and breaking contact decisively. The groan had been more of a moan, to be honest, and it had sounded undeniably wanton.

Crosby could blame the kiss on Darren, or the scene, or temporary insanity. But the sound he'd let out made it all too clear he liked having Darren's tongue in his mouth. And that was something he couldn't explain away.

He scrambled backwards, his knee hitting the computer and snapping it shut. Everything in him was screaming to retreat, but there was nowhere to go in this prison of a hotel room, unless he hid in the bathroom. He squeezed his eyes shut, centering himself using his familiar method. Slowly, he opened them to find Darren hadn't moved. Crosby wasn't sure what he was going to find on his face, but he forced himself to look.

Darren wore a semblance of his usual insouciant grin, but it didn't match his eyes, which were a little glazed, a little dazed. He looked...confused. Well, that made two of them.

Crosby didn't think, just spoke. "Why did you do that?"

Darren hesitated, then said, "It was in the script."

Crosby could have let him have the out, but he was feeling too raw to let it slide. "Grady's supposed to kiss Hank, not the other way around."

"I got caught up in it, I guess. You're good. You're going to kill at your audition."

Crosby didn't 100 percent buy what Darren was feeding him, but if it was true, if he'd only been playing his part, improvising a little, then that meant he hadn't actually been kissing Darren at all. Darren had only been acting.

And Crosby was screwed.

His stomach ached as disappointment flooded his gut. Of course, Darren wasn't attracted to an unfriendly, pompous actor who'd made his life difficult when they were teenagers.

"Thanks for reading with me, I guess," Crosby said, trying not to let his hurt show. "I'm going to—" He was going to say take a shower, desperate for some measure of privacy, but Darren didn't let him finish.

"Actually, that's a lie. I mean, yeah, I was playing

Hank, and Hank really wanted Grady to kiss him. So, I might have taken the initiative. Sorry." Darren was actually blushing, a rosy flush spreading beneath his eyes, which were darting everywhere except Crosby. "But then I realized I was kissing *you*, and somehow, I couldn't stop. It felt really fucking good."

Crosby didn't know what to say. Okay, it assuaged his ego to know Darren had liked it. But that didn't mean Darren wanted to do it again. Crosby wasn't even sure he wanted to do it again. He'd had his share of one-time hook-ups, but Darren wasn't someone he could kiss without consequences. Clearly.

"You're really, um," Darren coughed nervously, "attractive. Is it weird I said that?"

Darren being nervous was so disorienting, Crosby didn't know what to do.

In the face of Crosby's silence, Darren rambled on. "I mean, it's not like I don't know what you look like. And you've always been—" He gestured to Crosby's body, and since Crosby had had people objectifying him since he was fourteen, he understood what Darren meant. He felt more self-conscious at this moment than the time he'd posed shirtless with a horse and cowboy hat for some dumb magazine spread he'd instantly regretted.

"—but I didn't *know*, know. You know? And I can't help wishing I'd known earlier. Except you have this thing about not dating your co-workers. Which is totally levelheaded. Unless maybe you'd make an exception for a weird snowstorm-induced one-night stand?"

Crosby stared at him, agog. A one-night stand with Darren was his dream—and his worst nightmare.

"I'm kidding," Darren said quickly, though neither of them thought he'd been kidding. "Unless you're into it. Ha ha." He actually said the words "ha ha," then lapsed into an embarrassed chuckle.

Crosby was facing another one of those crossroads. The choice on one hand to play along, to maintain the status quo, to keep everything locked down as tightly as he had for fifteen years. On the other hand, he could choose to take the leap. To dare to tell the truth, freeing himself from his own rules and restrictions.

He gathered all his courage and took another plunge into the cold, icy waters of truth.

"I can't have a one-night stand with you," he said deliberately, imbuing his words with meaning. "I don't think I could be with you like that." His brain flashed unhelpful images of him and Darren in bed together, rolling around in the sheets like some soft-core porn clip, and he swallowed against a wave of desire.

"I couldn't do it and then walk away. I know myself. It would, well, it would be too hard to have something I've fantasized about for so long and have to pretend it meant nothing. To have to see you, not to mention work with you, and know it was meaningless to you. I'm not cut out for that."

Darren's eyes were fixed on him, getting wider with each damning word. "Shit."

"Yeah." Crosby smiled unhappily. "Sorry. About everything."

"No, it's okay," Darren rushed to say. "I mean. No one's ever said anything like that to me before."

"I know I probably made this situation even weirder," he said. "Nothing about this weekend is what you wanted—"

"Hey, I don't think you're exactly an expert on what I do or don't want," Darren said quickly.

Crosby breathed through the stab of hurt. "Right. Anyway. It's okay. At least it's all out there now, and we don't have to pretend anymore."

"So when you say it's all out there...what exactly is out there?"

"Just, uh, you know. That whole thing about my stupid crush and that I, you know. Don't not like you." This was excruciating. Next time he thought the truth would set him free, he'd bite his tongue in half before baring his soul.

"Okay, to be totally, a hundred percent clear. When you say you don't not like me, you mean you actually do like me?"

Crosby rolled his eyes.

"No, I'm serious, Crosby. I've spent years believing you thought I was as undesirable as a piece of chewing gum on the bottom of your Chuck Taylors. There's still an adjustment going on."

How many times was Darren going to want to hear it? Was he ever going to let this go? Crosby sighed. "I told you; it was easier to act as if I didn't like you than to constantly make sure I didn't let you know how very much I did."

"You did what?" Darren asked—the sadist.

"I liked you," Crosby ground out between clenched teeth.

Darren's sudden grin flashed neon-bright. "Now, was that so hard?"

Crosby wouldn't give him the satisfaction of letting on just how hard it was. "Can we go to bed now?"

Darren shrugged. "I'd definitely be up for that, but it sounds like it's not on the table."

Wait. What? "I meant, I'm going to bed. In my bed. Alone."

"Got it."

Darren didn't move as Crosby rose, put his computer in its case, then detoured by his stuff to grab something to sleep in. Good thing they were going home tomorrow—he was definitely out of clean clothes.

"I'm going to take a shower."

Darren nodded. "I think I'll take one in the morning. Better turn in if we're going to get up early enough to dig out the cars before the storm part two."

"I'll set an alarm," Crosby offered.

"Thanks."

"Well, good night, then."

Darren smiled, as if no revelations had occurred, as if they hadn't been kissing a few minutes ago. As if he hadn't issued a quasi-joking invitation for meaningless sex.

"Goodnight, Crosby."

Crosby shouldn't be disappointed. He'd confessed, and it hadn't ruined anything. Darren was still being friendly to him, and he could at last be more relaxed around a guy he normally felt tense around. These were all good things. Tomorrow, they'd part ways and probably not see each other again for months. Nothing had truly changed, except Darren knew how Crosby felt.

And Crosby knew what he tasted like.

He slipped into the bathroom, turned on the shower in the sleek, glassed-in stall. A lot of the larger rooms in the inn had a bathtub as well, but this room only had a shower, albeit a very nice shower.

Once under the steaming spray, he allowed himself a small, private freakout. He'd kissed *Darren Silverstein*. Darren Silverstein had kissed *him*. They'd *kissed*.

It had felt weird, and wonderful. Crosby was an idiot for turning down what could have been an amazing night.

He touched his lips, trying to memorize the way they'd felt moving against Darren's. The idea that he'd never have that again—honestly, it was a depressing thought.

Still, his heart was surprisingly light as he grabbed the soap. Shy, scared teenage Crosby, who thought Darren Silverstein was the coolest, hottest guy ever, would have given him a high-five if he were there right now. Crosby supposed, in a way, he was. He grinned, happy on behalf of his teenage self. Sure, he was a complete dork, but so what?

He'd grown up some tonight, maybe even achieved some closure. So he and Darren would never be a thing. They'd shared a moment, though. They understood each other better. And Crosby would find someone just as cool and hot as Darren someday, and Darren would probably be super happy for him, because that's the kind of guy he was.

He ignored the tiny slice of him that still desperately wanted that guy to be Darren and washed his hair.

# Chapter Ten



Darren pretended to be asleep when Crosby came out of the bathroom. He didn't trust himself to see him backlit, the bathroom light silhouetting the curve of his cheek or the breadth of his shoulders. Not now that he knew what it felt like to kiss him. He kept his eyes shut, but he couldn't shut out the sounds of Crosby preparing for bed, sliding under the covers mere feet away. He seemed restless, rustling his sheets for what seemed a long time before he finally settled.

Darren opened his eyes when silence finally fell,

feeling wide awake despite their earlier outdoor adventure in the snow and emotional revelations of the night. It wasn't every day you discovered a guy you thought hated you actually liked you. It wasn't every day a guy as hot as Spencer Crosby let Darren kiss him. And it definitely wasn't a common occurrence for Darren to suggest a hookup and get shot down.

He didn't mind that Crosby had turned him down. He had every right, not to mention Crosby's unassailable point about them working together. If Darren was going to direct *Sawyer's Cove* in the future, a one-night stand wasn't necessarily the best decision. But that presupposed feelings would be hurt. Which meant feelings would be involved. And Darren had had plenty of no-feelings-involved one-night stands. But Crosby's feelings clearly wouldn't be left at the hotel-room door. Even if he hadn't specified exactly how *much* he liked Darren, he'd unambiguously said a onetime hookup was a deal breaker.

Which left Darren's gut churning. He felt like he did in third grade when Emily Cohen had sent him a Valentine on which she'd scrawled, "will you be my boyfriend?" Eight-year-old Darren didn't want to be anyone's boyfriend, let alone Emily Cohen's. He'd felt guilty and embarrassed and eventually wrote her a nice note about how he wasn't looking for a girlfriend, but she was super nice and thanks, anyway. She'd never been quite as friendly to him after.

This wasn't exactly the same situation. Crosby, at least, was the right gender. But there was still a bubbling, nervous feeling inside him he associated with being wanted and not knowing what to do about it.

Spencer Crosby *like*-liked him. He liked him enough not to want to sleep with him with no strings. And it had been a very long time since Darren had been faced with someone who liked him that much.

He should have been relieved Crosby was being the grown-up. They were free to be friends and let the bad blood between them fade away. They could help each other's careers and cheer each other on—part of the big, happy family that was the *Sawyer's Cove* cast and crew, past and present.

But he felt jumpy, itchy in his skin. The bedsheets felt scratchy, when he knew for a fact they were soft 800-thread-count cotton. He was overly hot in his sweats and T-shirt. He pushed down the comforter, thought about taking off his shirt. Why had he worn one to bed, anyway?

His eyes, accustomed to the dark, made out Spencer's form in the other bed. He really was easy on the eyes, even asleep, with soft lashes and golden hair. He looked like a Renaissance angel painted with egg tempura he vaguely remembered learning about the time he'd gone to the Uffizi in Florence. Cinematographers loved Crosby, his translucent skin, his sharp cheekbones, his luminescent green eyes all responding to light as if he was born to be committed to film.

And those lips, so full and mouthwatering. Darren's cock was filling out, thinking about Crosby's mouth, how it felt on his, so warm and wet. It was an easy leap to imagine what it would feel like to slide his dick in-between those bee stung lips and have Crosby suck him down.

Fuck. He should not be thinking about this, not least because he wanted to touch himself, and that was totally inappropriate, especially given their earlier conversation.

He turned over, away from Crosby's sleeping outline. What was happening to him? He felt out of control with hormones and desire. He blamed Crosby, naturally, for reminding him what it was like to be young and dumb, full of confusing need and utterly uncertain of how you were ever going to get anything close to what you wanted.

Crosby saying what he'd wanted was Darren himself was world changing.

Made painfully obvious by the persistent erection he couldn't will away, it was Darren's turn to want.

Maybe the whirling in his gut was because he wasn't put off by Crosby's admission or by his apparent feelings for Darren. To the contrary, he liked it. He was turned on by Crosby's feelings. By Crosby himself.

Darren wanted Spencer Crosby with shocking intensity.

He rolled to face Crosby. A hot, decent guy three feet away, and he couldn't do anything about it because—why? It would mean too much? He wasn't an asshole; it wasn't like he was going to sleep with Crosby and never talk to him again. But what was the alternative? If they started sleeping together—what—would it turn into a regular thing? Friends with benefits? Crosby had implied that wasn't something he was interested in. What did that leave?

Darren forced himself to mentally form the words. A real relationship. Dating. The possibility of love. Commitment.

He shivered. He'd suspected he was ready for something more serious, but actually contemplating such a relationship was more than a little terrifying. He might be getting tired of fucking around with guys he couldn't see a future with, but he wasn't exactly ready to get married and settle down tomorrow.

Not that Crosby said he wanted to get married or anything. He only said he couldn't do a one-night stand. But what if Darren offered him something else? What if they spent more time together, tried to see if there was something between them they could build on?

Of course, exploratory dating was all well and good when it was some random guy from a dating app. If it didn't work out, they could go their separate ways. He and Crosby had lots of mutual friends—what would they think if they were dating? Ariel would probably be over the moon about it. Nash would be happy for them, too.

Darren shook himself. Was he thinking about this as a real possibility? What if it went wrong? What if they tried it and it was a disaster and then they had to work together, and Crosby's feigned attitude of indifference and apathy turned into actual enmity?

What if they couldn't stay friends and it wrecked the show?

On the other hand, if it worked, it could be incredible.

How could he know before putting their tentative friendship on the line? He was up for taking risks when it was a job he really wanted or he was betting on a hand of poker. He was surprisingly adept at bluffing.

But as much as he loved games, this was too real. And it might be too risky.

As he stared at Crosby, something shifted in his chest. Crosby was worth taking a chance on, no matter how badly it turned out in the end. He was the kind of guy you threw caution to the wind for, because being with him would be an unforgettable ride, even if you ended up overturned in a muddy ditch.

And damn, he was aching to take Crosby for a ride.

Decision made, he rolled off his mattress onto the narrow strip of carpet between the two beds. He shuffled forward on his knees to Crosby's side, reached up, and turned on the reading lamp. Crosby's thick blond eyebrows twitched in sleep, but he didn't wake up. Darren drank him in for a minute, feeling the moment spool out into the future, wondering if this was only the first of thousands of times he'd see Crosby sleeping. He couldn't shake the premonition that this was their future, that they were going to be spending much more time together, years even. Maybe the rest of their lives.

Or maybe he just really wanted to get laid by the hottest guy in Misty Harbor.

"Crosby." He put a hand lightly on Crosby's shoulder, felt the soft T-shirt over hard muscle.

"Hmm?" Crosby's striking eyes flickered open. "Something wrong?"

Darren shook his head. "No. I wanted to ask you something."

Crosby frowned and peered at the bedside clock. "It's one-thirty in the morning."

"It is?" Darren was genuinely shocked. He'd been lying in bed for hours, and it hardly felt like any time had passed since Crosby had dropped off to sleep. "Shit. Sorry."

"What is it?"

Darren's courage faltered. "What if—" He really hadn't thought this through. He remembered Emily Cohen and fell back on the language of third grade. "What if I said I, um, liked you back?"

Crosby didn't make fun of him for his juvenile diction. Instead, he seemed to shrink in on himself. "You don't have to do this."

"No, I, um. I think this could be really good. I mean, I don't know. But I want to try. Would you take a chance on me? On us?"

"Us?" Crosby whispered. He sounded a little dazed.

Darren supposed he couldn't blame him for being out of it. He'd been rudely woken up by his slightly deranged roommate and was being asked to make important life decisions. Still, he was too far committed now to let this go. He leaned forward another few inches until his chest pressed against the side of Crosby's bed.

"Could we try being together and see what's there?"

"I don't—"

Darren didn't want to experience the disappointment of being turned down by Crosby a second time. "Look, you're awesome. I'm awesome. We have a lot in common. We're attracted to each other. And you said you didn't not like me. I don't not like you, too. Very much."

"Really?" This time, he sounded less dazed and more hopeful.

"Really." Darren smiled. "And I really want to kiss you again. Can I?"

"Is this a dream?" Crosby said, his smile disarmingly innocent. "Am I going to wake up in the morning and you won't remember any of this?"

"Not a dream, and maybe we can wake up together," Darren said, liking the idea of it. "Can I get in with you?"

There was a protracted moment when Crosby didn't move, and Darren was suspended in judgment. He held his breath. Finally, Crosby scooted backward, leaving a bare spot on the mattress for Darren to slip into, warm from Crosby's body heat. That minor intimacy had Darren's cock hardening up again. He hadn't been this responsive to a guy in forever.

Crosby spread the comforter over Darren, propped up on his elbow, while Darren lay against the pillows. He didn't know what to do next. They were inches apart, the only light from the reading lamp. Should he turn it off? But he wanted to see Crosby. Though if they were kissing, his eyes would be closed.

He let out a huff of a laugh. "Sorry. I'm not usually this inept." He glanced up, and Crosby was looking down at him through long, gold-tipped lashes.

"It's okay," Crosby said.

He put one large, warm hand on Darren's hip, then scooted forward so the lower half of their bodies were pressed together. Darren felt Crosby's cock pressed against his hip, which meant Crosby could certainly feel how hard Darren was through their flimsy sweats. He flushed, oddly shy. But why shouldn't Crosby know how much he wanted him?

Crosby moved first, nudging Darren's cheek with his nose, until he tipped his head up and they could slot their mouths together. That was familiar, a delicious meeting that had Darren positively aching for more. Crosby again went first, pressing the tip of his tongue to the seam of Darren's lips. He let him inside, both of them emitting out small, grateful noises as their kiss deepened.

It was sweltering under the covers, but Crosby's mouth was hotter. Darren needed to get his shirt off immediately. He stopped kissing Crosby long enough to haul his shirt up and off, and figured he might as well lose his sweats while he was at it. He kicked them off, leaving him in his boxers. Crosby watched him, an amused smirk on his face.

"What?"

"Eager?" Crosby drawled.

"Fuck, yes."

He dove back in, feeling more in control now,

wondering if Crosby would give up leading for a while. He pushed him back on the pillows, attacking his mouth and jaw and the side of his perfect neck, tasting soap-clean skin, and smelling the inn's signature shampoo. Crosby arched up obediently when Darren shoved his shirt up, and then they were chest-to-chest, rubbing against each other a little frantically, as if each was certain the other might disappear if they stopped moving.

"You feel good," Darren murmured into Crosby's neck as he skimmed his hands down the other man's sides, over his pecs and peaked nipples, over his flat stomach and the soft, fine hair dusting the path from his navel to the waistband of the sweats Darren had lent him.

He let his fingers sneak under the edge, expecting to encounter the boxer briefs he'd seen him in yesterday when he'd made him do that silly dare to get ice in his underwear, but there was nothing beneath, just more hair, then Darren's fingers encountered the spongy head of an erect cock pointing straight toward him.

He yanked his hand back, but Crosby chuckled. "It's okay, Darren. You can touch me."

"Yeah. Of course, sorry." Darren was acting like a virgin on prom night. Maybe Crosby would get tired of his fumbling and decide he wasn't worth it. With renewed focus, Darren found the prize, wrapping his hand around Crosby's girth, acquainting himself with the weight and heft of him. He was dying to see what it looked like, but contented himself with stroking him from base to tip inside his sweats while he plied Crosby's neck and chest with kisses.

"Yeah, like that," Crosby said when he sped up. "Darren. Do we have any lube?"

Darren tried to keep up the rhythm and consider the question at the same time. "Uh. I don't think so. I didn't exactly plan on having sex on this trip."

"Yeah, me either," Crosby said. "I have condoms, but no lube. I just like it, um, wetter."

"Oh, right." Darren thought. They could use lotion, maybe? Or he could switch out his hand for his mouth. Saliva sprang into his mouth at the thought, right on cue. "Can I blow you?"

Crosby straight up whimpered, and Darren grinned. "I'll take that as a yes."

"You don't have to," Crosby said, but even he wasn't that good of an actor.

Darren kissed him one more time. "I want to," he said. "I give good head, I promise."

"Okay," Crosby said, and he shimmied out of his sweats, giving Darren his first glimpse at his uncovered cock, thick and rosy red, perfectly proportioned to the rest of Crosby's body. He was the golden mean brought to life.

"You're really unfairly gorgeous," Darren said, getting into position at the base of the bed while Crosby shifted the other way, propping himself up on pillows so he could presumably watch while Darren got to work.

"You think so?" Crosby sounded doubtful for some reason. "I didn't think I was your type."

"Huh? What's my type?"

Crosby's cheeks went scarlet. "I don't know."

"Come on, you've obviously given this some thought." If they were maybe going to see if there was something real between them, Darren couldn't be giving him free passes.

"Well, like Chris, or that one guy you were dating the last season of the old show—Javier?"

Darren had to think for a minute. "Oh yeah, Javier. I forgot about him."

"Well, they're both big, masculine guys. I figured that's what you like."

"Honey, you're definitely masculine," Darren said, eyeing Crosby's shoulders, his flat pecs, his perfect dick. At the same time, he knew what Crosby meant. Crosby was somehow softer than those guys, more curves. More beautiful. Not exactly a turnoff. "And I'm really, really attracted to you. Can I show you how much I want you?"

# Chapter Eleven



Darren licked his lips, leaving them wet and shiny. Crosby loved shiny things.

His entire body tightened at the implication that Darren was about to show him how much he wanted him by giving him head. Crosby also had a clue from the fact that Darren had been hard since he first got into Crosby's bed. He reeled at the knowledge of Darren's obvious desire.

But what Darren had said about them taking a chance and finding out if there could be something between them had him even more off-kilter. He couldn't believe he was about to potentially fuck it all up when they'd already passed out of the friend zone and into hookup territory, but he had to be sure.

"Darren, wait—you aren't doing this just because you think I want to, right?"

Sure, he believed Darren was attracted to him, but was all the "I like you" stuff a line to get him into bed? Or to get Darren into his bed, in this case?

Darren sat back on his heels, boxers still tented promisingly. "I may be a people pleaser, but I'm not pathological about it. It's been a long time since I slept with someone to make them like me. Besides," he added knowingly, "you already admitted to liking me. I'm just meeting you where you're at."

A few minutes ago, Darren said they had a lot in common. Crosby had never dated anyone who understood the privilege of being a working actor while being acutely aware of its drawbacks. The people Crosby tended to date were attracted to the perceived glamour of his job, then annoyed by his long hours and frequent travel.

He and Darren did have a lot in common, as different as they were. It seemed one thing they had in common, as wild as it might have seemed forty-eight hours ago, was mutual attraction.

Crosby relented. They were both adults, after all. Even if they fucked and came to their senses in the morning, they'd deal with the consequences like grown-ups.

Besides, his natural reserve crumbled in the face of Darren practically drooling at his feet, black hair spiked up all over the place, skin flushed, boyishly handsome and sexy at the same time.

He'd made mistakes in his life, but turning down sex with Darren Silverstein for a second time was not going to be one of them.

"I believe you."

Darren grinned, and Crosby's heart sent a fresh round of blood to his cheeks. Being on the receiving end of one of Darren's happy grins was intoxicating.

"You wanna take off your—" He gestured to Darren's crotch.

Darren's answer was to slide his shorts off to reveal his jutting erection. Crosby drank him in, dark curls, long, cut cock that made Crosby want all manner of things. He wanted very much to get acquainted with every part of Darren's anatomy, especially that part of him. He could easily imagine Darren opening him with his expressive fingers, then filling him up with his pretty cock. But he might actually pass out if Darren attempted to fuck him right now. He might not even survive this blow job, assuming Darren ever got around to giving him one.

As if reading his mind, Darren straddled Crosby's legs. He rubbed their cocks together, and they kissed again. There was still not enough slickness for his preference, but Darren still felt amazing writhing against him, their bodies learning each other's shape and feel.

The more they kissed, the more aroused Crosby became, and the fuzzier his brain got. Everything was hazy with the unreality of the hour; it was as if Crosby still hadn't fully woken up. He gave himself over to what was happening, grateful to stop overthinking and simply enjoy.

Darren slipped down his body and finally took Crosby's dick into his mouth. He lost the plot for a while, giving himself over to the pleasure of being given a blow job by someone who knew what he was doing. Darren hadn't sold himself short—he was good at giving head, enthusiastic and ambitious, able to take Crosby nearly to the root while getting his hands in on the action, gripping hips, thighs, cupping his balls, sliding a finger behind to press on his taint, pushing against his hole so the combination of pressure there and the suction on his dick had Crosby coming before he could issue a warning.

But Darren didn't seem to mind, just took it, pulling off and spitting discreetly into a tissue before crawling up Crosby's body to kiss him, all salty and musky. He stroked himself to completion in Crosby's lap, shooting gratifyingly quickly between their bellies.

They were both sweaty and sticky when Darren rolled off, padded to the bathroom, and returned with a wet washcloth. Crosby was surprised—he was usually the one who ended up doing the clean-up—but it was nice being looked after for a change.

Something on Darren's hip caught Crosby's attention as he wiped himself down.

"Wait, is that a tattoo?"

Darren peered down at himself, as if to confirm. "Yep." He twisted to show off his left hip.

Crosby leaned forward to make out the small black line drawing. It was a remarkably delicate, highly detailed tattoo of a winged insect. "You said you didn't have one."

"No, I said I didn't have a tattoo of a butterfly. That is a cecropia moth."

"Why a moth?"

"Moths are excellent pollinators. They're beautiful. I like them."

"Huh." He'd never given moths much thought, but if Darren was interested in them, he'd read an entire book about them. There were surely some interesting podcasts he could listen to on the subject.

"You got any ink?" Darren asked, tossing the washcloth onto a pile of dirty clothes.

"No," Crosby said. "I never wanted to cause issues for the makeup teams."

"Very thoughtful," Darren said, handing him his sweats. "That's why I picked this spot. Not too disruptive."

Crosby reached out to touch the mark on Darren's bare skin. He marveled at being able to touch him at all. "Nice. I like it."

"I like *you*," Darren said, pulling on his boxers. He

could have been joking, or facetious, but Crosby thought he was being serious.

Crosby tried to sort out how he felt about Darren liking him. He'd said it a couple of times now, and it was getting easier each time to believe him. Still, call him an insecure actor but, "Why?"

"I don't know," Darren said unhurriedly, as if he was trying to work it out himself. "I think it's because you're even asking me why, when two days ago I would have assumed you'd be full of reasons why you should be adored. And that was never fair of me, no matter what attitude you gave off. So, I'm sorry."

Darren shouldn't have to take responsibility for Crosby's own shortcomings. "It's okay. I didn't make it easy to be around me or get to know me. I'm sorry."

"It's all right." Darren stood beside the bed, leaned over, and kissed him as casually as if he did it every day. "Also, that was fucking hot, and I can't wait to do it again."

Crosby glowed with the praise. Darren had enjoyed having sex with him. It was his teenage fantasy come true. He wondered how long it would be before he found out where the catch was.

He thought Darren might go back to his own bed for half a second, but he flopped down on the bed next to Crosby, clicked off the light, and settled into the crook of Crosby's arm.

It felt so good, Crosby tensed. Was this too fast?

Darren must have sensed his apprehension. He turned around in Crosby's arms and whispered, "I like you, Crosby." The words were a sardonic play on the traditional bedtime "I love you," but even so, they felt genuine.

Crosby smiled into the dark, allowing himself to be soothed. He let his muscles go lax. "I like you, too."

And he fell asleep with Darren's comforting weight at his side.

# Chapter Twelve



The persistent chirp of his alarm brought Crosby out of a dead sleep. He opened his eyes only far enough to jab the button on his phone where it lay on the night table closest to the window, then rolled over and encountered a body.

His eyes flew all the way open, his heart beating double time until he remembered who else was in his bed.

Darren's eyes were squeezed shut like a little kid feigning sleep. "Turn it off. Too early."

He sounded grumpy as a little kid, too.

Crosby smiled. "It's off. But we should probably get up and get a move on. Check out's at eleven."

"Tired," Darren said, still without opening his eyes.

"Maybe that's because you stayed up until the middle of the night, then decided to seduce me."

Darren's lips curved up. "I did do that, didn't I?" Slowly, he cracked open his eyes. Crosby glimpsed gray behind thick black lashes. "Worth it."

Crosby let out a heavy breath. Okay. It wasn't all in his head. It wasn't a dream. He and Darren had sex, slept all night in the same bed, and now Darren was flirting with him. Somehow his life had taken a turn, and while he thought distantly he should be concerned they were moving too fast, it was hard to be worried when the guy of his dreams was nuzzling his shoulder and peppering his arm with light kisses.

"I want to kiss you," Darren said as he worked his way down to Crosby's wrist, "but morning breath."

"Fair," Crosby said, not offended. He knew Darren was probably worried more about his own breath than Crosby's. He was the one who'd had a cock in his mouth last night, after all.

*Damn.* The memory of being sucked off by Darren was getting him going again. He palmed himself through his sweatpants until his hand was knocked aside by Darren's.

Darren stroked him a few times through his pants. "You want a repeat performance?"

"No, that's okay," Crosby said reluctantly. It would have been incredibly selfish to accept another blow job when he hadn't yet returned the favor. Never let it be said he wasn't a gentleman. "Wanna take a shower together?"

"Is there room?" Darren asked doubtfully.

"It might be tight, but we'll make it fit." Crosby surprised himself by winking. He could flirt, too, apparently.

Darren laughed, and the warm sound made Crosby even harder. Making Darren laugh was almost as satisfying as an orgasm.

"Saucy," Darren said. "Sure, let's get all soapy and slippery."

"But then we really have to get moving," Crosby reminded him. "I don't want to be stuck on the turnpike in the snow."

"Yeah, your roadster isn't exactly four-wheel drive," Darren agreed. "Fine, fine. We'll be quick."

They did fit in the shower, barely. They playfully jockeyed for space and got soaped up, catching each other's mouths in kisses—morning breath be damned—every time they traded spots under the showerhead.

When they were clean, and both thoroughly aroused, Crosby shut the water off, sank to his knees, and guided Darren's dick to his mouth. Crosby watched Darren, whose gaze never left Crosby's face—his eyebrows slanted in concentration. He got used to the feel of the other man's cock, loving the fresh taste of him, digging his hands into the meat of Darren's thighs and not minding his stinging knees on the hard tile.

Darren traced Crosby's distended lips with his fingers, reverence in his touch and awe in his eyes. Crosby sucked him hard, then pulled off, jerking him once, twice, until he groaned and spilled, a jet of come catching Crosby on the chin.

Joining him on the shower floor, Darren sank down, licked Crosby's chin clean, then plunged his tongue into his mouth, bitter and salty and so fucking hot, Crosby thought he might come from that alone. But then Darren took his hand, still covered with come, and guided it to Crosby's own cock, keeping his hand on top.

Together, they jerked him off, using come as lube. That did make him blow, harder than he should have, considering he'd had an explosive orgasm only a few hours before.

When they were again sticky and spent, they laughed and turned the shower back on, rinsing away the evidence, trading lazy kisses under the hot water until Crosby felt like his lips might end up permanently chapped.

Darren didn't seem to be in any hurry to turn off the water and get on with their day. He hadn't stopped touching Crosby since they woke up, and it didn't make Crosby feel smothered or trapped. He felt...happy. Uncomplicatedly, unreservedly happy.

Oh, dear.

He stiffened and reached past Darren to shut the tap off. He had been in enough network dramas to know this was usually when his character got a rude awakening. This feeling couldn't last.

"Hey, something wrong?" Darren asked.

Crosby retreated, reaching for a fluffy white towel and passing it to Darren first, then grabbing one for himself.

"No." *Not yet.* "Should we order breakfast?"

"Good idea. Same as yesterday?"

"Sure."

Darren went to make the call, and Crosby dried off, looking at himself in the mirror. He had beard burn on the side of his neck from Darren's stubble, and his eyes were slightly bloodshot from the lack of sleep.

He still couldn't wrap his head around what was happening. Were they a couple now? Neither of them wanted something casual, but they'd only just started to be friends, which was, granted, all his fault.

Could they skip the friends stage and go right to being lovers? He supposed that's how it worked if you were dating someone you'd just met. His parents had definitely been a love-at-first-sight situation, if he believed the stories they told about late 1980s New York. His father had been ascending in the theater world for a decade already. His mother, twelve years his junior, had been getting her first parts. They met at a cast party and fell for each other right away, barely leaving each other's side in the next thirty-five years, to the detriment of his mother's career, which turned out to be rather short-lived.

The Crosby/Van Wycks apparently imprinted on

their one true love and didn't look back. Could the same have been true for Crosby? Was it possible he'd met the love of his life as a seventeen-year-old?

Did he love Darren?

*Pump the brakes, Crosby.* They were two guys in their early thirties. Maybe they weren't chasing anonymous flings anymore, but that didn't mean they had to move so fast.

He toweled off his hair, and finger combed it, since the complimentary comb from the inn wasn't going to work on his curls. As unexpectedly fun as this enforced stay had been, it would be nice to get home to his stuff, including his hair products and wardrobe. His plants probably needed watering, and he had to prepare for his audition, only a few days away now.

He really wanted this part. And despite the unconventional way his line reading with Darren had gone, he thought he had a good handle on the scene. Rehearsing with someone else, someone as talented as Darren, had really helped.

Darren knew his stuff—as both an actor and a director. Maybe they could practice again together before the audition—once they were back in New York.

New York. They were supposed to go home today. Crosby's chest burned with a spike of anxiety. What if what they were feeling for each other was only because of the storm and the hotel room? What if, once outside the bubble of the Misty Harbor Inn, Darren realized he didn't like Crosby much after all? He had the choice of anyone in the five boroughs. Why would he want Crosby? Difficult, closed off, shy Crosby who'd lied to him the entire time they'd known each other?

A knock came on the bathroom door. "Did you fall in? Breakfast is here. I bribed them to expedite it for us."

"Sorry, be right out." He wrapped the towel around his waist tightly and opened the door.

Darren was dressed and setting up the room service cart between their two beds. He looked up when Crosby came out and went over to his clothes, pulling on his cleanest everything.

"Coffee?"

"Please."

When he was dressed, he noticed Darren had set the plates next to each other, so they'd have to sit side by side on one bed, instead of across from each other like yesterday. He smiled and joined Darren on the edge of the bed.

"You're quiet," Darren said around a mouthful of toast. "Did I do something wrong?"

"No." Jesus, Crosby was fucking this up already. "No, I...I get quiet when I'm thinking."

"I noticed," Darren said, a smile in his voice. "Can I ask what you're thinking about?"

Crosby was unsettled to realize Darren actually cared about what was going on in Crosby's head. That's what friends did. What boyfriends did. Suddenly, the stakes seemed entirely too high to answer the question.

Darren was gazing at him with his clear eyes, no agenda hiding in them, no impatience, no judgment.

"I'm—scared." He blinked. That wasn't at all what he thought he was going to say.

Darren swallowed his bite of toast noisily, reached for his coffee cup, and took a huge sip.

Crosby immediately tried to backtrack. "Shit. I'm sorry. I don't know what's the matter with me. It's like this room has some kind of truth curse on it. I can't seem to not tell you what I'm thinking and feeling, and it's totally out of character. You don't need to deal with my issues." He took a sip of his own coffee and winced. It was too hot.

Darren put his cup down and turned to face Crosby. "Hey, first of all, I'm glad you're being honest. You're being brave. I can't help—" He stopped, seemed to think better of what he was going to say, and then reconsidered again. "Fuck it. I can't help wishing you'd told me how you felt ages ago. We can't change the past, and I guess things worked out the way they were supposed to. But maybe things would have been even better if we'd explored this earlier."

"I probably would have fucked it up," Crosby said miserably. "Like I'm probably going to fuck this up, too."

"Hey, give yourself some credit. Keep being honest with me, and I'll keep being honest with you, and that's half the battle right there." Darren put a reassuring hand on Crosby's thigh and squeezed.

"So it doesn't freak you out that I'm scared?"

"I guess it depends. What are you scared about?"

Crosby looked at Darren, a little rumpled, his hair uncombed. They'd had sex, twice, and Crosby couldn't wait to get his hands on him again. He wanted to bring him home to the city and take him to his favorite restaurants and meet Darren's friends and introduce him to his parents. He wanted them to be happy. Together.

"I'm scared because this feels really right, but what if it's all a storm-induced illusion? What if we get back to New York and you change your mind? I've wanted you for so long, and now I have you, apparently. But what if you never feel the same way about me? I'm scared I'm going to get my heart broken."

He made himself watch Darren's reaction to that little bombshell. Darren's eyes widened a fraction, but he didn't move his hand off Crosby's thigh.

"I know that's heavy and a lot to put on you, and I'm being childish and—"

"It's not childish, it's romantic," Darren interrupted. He snapped his fingers and grinned excitedly. "That's it! You're a total romantic."

"Yeah," Crosby said sadly. "It's a problem."

Darren leaned over, kissed him soundly on the mouth. "It's sexy."

"Yeah?" He wasn't convinced.

"Yeah. And you're right, I don't feel the same way about you that you feel about me. And it's a little scary." Darren scooted closer, so they were hip to hip. "I don't know what's going to happen when we get back to New York, either. But we can't live in this hotel room for the rest of our lives. What I do know is, I like you. A lot. And I'm willing to take a chance. We're smart enough to figure this out."

"You make it sound so simple."

"It is simple." Darren kissed him again. It was hard to remember all the reasons he should be anxious when Darren was kissing him. "We're going to be fine. We'll take it one step at a time. Now eat your eggs."

Crosby took a half-hearted bite of his breakfast. Darren was right. But even if it was simpler than he was making it, he had a feeling it wouldn't exactly be easy.

# Chapter Thirteen

@sawyerscovedaily If Noah Rosen doesn't show up at some point in this season I am going to be so pissed. According to #thesawyerscoverewatch-projectpodcast, he was in Misty Harbor while they were shooting, but he hasn't been in any promo. I'm scared to hope! #noahrosen #justice-fornoahrosen #darrensilverstein #sawyerscove

Darren was not at all sure he hadn't made a huge mistake.

He'd given that big, optimistic speech to Crosby that morning about taking it one step at a time, and he'd believed himself. He'd tried to stick to it, to put one foot in front of the other and not get overwhelmed by the drastic upheaval in their relationship. He was allowed to look at Crosby all he wanted now—he was allowed to touch him. Allowed to joke and tease and Crosby actually liked it instead of rolling his eyes and keeping his distance. Crosby actually liked *him*.

It was an unsettlingly wonderful new normal, and it made it hard to keep his feet on the ground when he felt like floating up to the sky.

Still, they had practical matters to attend to. They kept their hands to themselves while they packed and checked out of the inn. He tried to get away with paying the bill in full, but Crosby insisted on splitting it with him. Then they dug out their cars. He'd been grateful for the gloves provided by Trevor, and the snow scrapers loaned by the inn.

His old, beat-up black Jeep fired right up after they cleared the snow from the windshield and driver's door, while Crosby's shiny silver sports car took longer to extricate. Still, they were soon ready to get on the road after a brief, self-conscious goodbye in the parking lot. Darren waited outside of Crosby's door, watching him buckle up and connect his phone to the stereo.

"I have a lot of podcasts to keep me company," Crosby said, his cheeks and nose cherry red from the cold.

Darren smiled, vaguely wishing they could drive back together. They could argue over which podcasts to listen to and which route to take. It didn't make sense to drive in tandem since Crosby was going to return the Battleship game and basket to Trevor on his way out of town.

Darren ducked his head through the open driver's

door window and kissed Crosby briefly. "Text me, and we'll meet up later."

Crosby nodded and vroomed off in his sporty coupe, looking like a dashing playboy prince, way above Darren's pay grade.

He climbed into his second-hand jalopy and spent the entire three-hour drive back to the city second-guessing himself. What had he gotten them into? He had no experience with long-term relationships, and he'd decided his first one should be with a guy who'd carried a torch for him for years.

*Brilliant choice, Darren.*

Then there was the very real fact that they worked together. They had two more seasons of *Sawyer's Cove* to shoot. There was as yet no guarantee Darren's character would be in more than one episode—but the cliffhanger ending for Noah and Will at the end of season one made Darren pretty sure he'd be coming back. And maybe he'd be back on set directing, too.

Crosby's no-dating-co-stars rule made a lot of sense. And Darren was making him break it. What if things didn't work out? Did that automatically make him the bad guy? Was he shooting his own career in the foot?

He didn't feel like he'd made such a bad decision whenever he remembered how Crosby had looked on his knees sucking him off in the shower, his pouty lips put to good use, his green eyes glittering with want. But they couldn't base their entire relationship on sex. Well, he guessed they could *try*, but he knew the wick would burn out fast and leave them burned out, too.

The snow that had fallen the past few days in the city had been shunted off to the side, turning the sidewalks into a slushy, dirty mess. He thanked the New York parking gods for the hundredth time that his apartment came with a garage spot. He parked and trundled up to his third-floor apartment with his overnight bag.

His apartment was overly warm and stuffy, so he cracked open a window. He took stock of the nearly empty fridge, realized he hadn't done laundry for a few days before he'd gone to Misty Harbor and the bed could stand to be stripped. He trundled to the basement to do a load, sorted through his mail on the way back up. He opened his computer, considered a grocery order. Should he get some things Crosby might like? What did he like?

He checked his phone, and there was still nothing. No calls, no texts. Wouldn't Crosby be back in the city by now? He glanced around his apartment. He liked it fine, but it was nothing special. He spent most of his time working, socializing, eating out. The lifestyle of a young, busy Manhattanite didn't usually involve spending a lot of time at home.

He got up, paced a little, trying to identify what he was feeling.

He missed Crosby.

He'd spent three days straight with the guy, and he wanted more. Shit. Maybe now *he* was scared. He was trying to decide if that was a good thing or a bad thing when his phone finally buzzed.

Do you have New Year's plans? I'm
thinking of throwing a game night.
Want in?

He latched onto the contact from the outside world and instead of texting her back hit the button to make a call.

"Hey, you," Ariel said, her deep, melodious voice familiar and grounding.

"Hey," Darren said. He'd followed the impulse to call her, but now that he had her on the phone, he wasn't sure what to say. He and Crosby hadn't exactly discussed if they were going to tell people about them. And Ariel wasn't a neutral party. She'd known them both forever.

"So, did you survive the night?" she asked when he didn't say anything.

"Huh?"

"You and Crosby? Clearly, he didn't kill you, but I'm assuming you didn't do anything you'd regret, either."

He choked on air. "We survived," he managed. "We ended up having to stay two nights. Just got home."

"Me, too. Sometimes I wish Misty Harbor was the tiniest bit closer to the city. Or at least had a good train there. So, game night?"

Game night made him think of Crosby. He imagined them showing up to Ariel's together, teaming up, and trouncing everyone else. Then they'd come home and team up again. For sex. He shook his head. One step at a time, he'd said. Why was it so hard not to rush headlong into this relationship?

"Are you there?" Ariel asked.

"Yeah, I'm here. Game night. Sounds good. Uh. I might bring someone. Okay with you?"

"Of course, the more, the merrier," she said, then her voice changed, and she said silkily, "Oh, like, *bring* bring someone? Who? Are you seeing someone?"

"Yeah, I am," he said. That much felt safe to share. "It's new. And I'm kind of freaking out."

"Why, darling?"

"Because this guy, he's really amazing and, like, a total one of one, you know what I mean? Not like anyone else. And he apparently really likes me, which is kind of unbelievable in the first place, but he does, and I really like him, but it's so new."

Ariel laughed. "I'm not seeing a problem, sweetie."

Darren barely heard her. "I mean, it's not like I could have fallen for him in two days, is it? That doesn't happen in real life. People don't fall in love overnight. I mean, what I'm feeling has gotta be lust, right? I've definitely fallen in lust pretty quickly, but that burns out. So maybe that's what this is. Except I don't just want to jump him, I want to talk to him and find out everything about him and cook for him, and he'd probably be a really good dad, because he's really serious and thoughtful, but he also has this playful side I didn't know about. Oh, and games. He loves games. And I do, too. So why am I freaking out?"

He sucked in a breath, feeling a little lightheaded after his rant.

"Breathe, honey," she said. "It sounds like you're

freaking out because you think this guy could be The One."

"The one?"

"Capital T, Capital O."

"Oh, The One." Could Crosby be the guy he'd been looking for all his life?

"Yeah, I know you know your *Sex and the City*."

"This isn't a TV show, Ariel; this is my life," he said, feeling a little bit like he wanted to cry.

"Okay, wow. This sounds major."

"That's what I'm saying!"

"So you like him. Maybe you even love him. And he likes you back. Congratulations. You want a medal?" No one did sassy like Ariel Tulip.

"I want to know it's all going to work out," he said. "My parents were happy until they weren't."

"You aren't your parents. And you and this guy sound like you're happy. You don't want to be happy?"

"Of course I want to be happy."

"So be happy with him. Nothing in life is guaranteed. Sounds like you got a good one. Enjoy and stop over-thinking it. You don't usually overthink things. That's Crosby's department." She laughed, and then her usually silvery laugh turned strangled. She coughed, sounding for a second like a cat with a furball.

Darren winced. She was too smart for her own good.

"You're not—you and *Crosby*?"

Darren let his silence be the answer.

She screeched, and he held the phone away from his ear to avoid damage to his eardrum. "Oh my heavens, this is incredible. You and Crosby—he has feelings for you? I knew there was some reason you two never got along, but I chalked it up to you being two very different people. But you like each other! And you're falling in love! And you're going to live happily ever after!" Predictably, Ariel sniffed. She cried at the drop of a hat.

"Calm down, please," Darren said, his own emotions in danger of spiraling. "I don't know, but also...yes?"

"This is so amazing. Another *Sawyer's Cove* romance. The fans are going to fucking lose their shit over this."

Darren froze. He hadn't thought about that, but she was right. "Look, it literally just happened. Please don't tell anyone. Crosby isn't really out. I didn't even know he was gay until the day before yesterday."

"You didn't? Jesus, your gaydar sucks. I knew the first time we met when he barely checked out my boobs."

"That certainly is a tell. You have very nice boobs," Darren said sincerely.

"Damn right I do. But of course I won't tell anyone. You two have to come to game night now. Good Lord, you two together...I never pictured it before, but you make a freaking adorable couple. You have to get a surrogate and have two babies so you can have one blond-haired, green-eyed, and one dark-haired, gray eyed. The prettiest babies ever."

"Okay, now you're getting way too invested in this." He wanted to be mortified, but he had to admit she was right.

"I am invested in this. I care about you both a lot.

And if you being together makes you happy, then it makes me very, very happy."

He laughed. "Thanks, Ariel. I'll endeavor to not screw it up."

"I believe in you."

"Thanks." He realized if he wanted to find out how Crosby was and what he was thinking, he should call him himself. "Count me in for game night. I'll see if Crosby's free."

"Okay. Love you, darling."

"Love you," he said, feeling lighter when he hung up.

She was right—he was overthinking things. He didn't know what was going to happen, but he had a hot, talented, clever guy to invite over, and that wasn't so bad. He found Crosby's number and hit send. Crosby picked up on the second ring.

"I just got home," he said. "Got caught up in some traffic in Stamford."

"Glad you made it safe," Darren said. "Wanna come over? I have no food, but I could order in."

"Now?" Crosby asked.

Darren lost a bit of his nerve. "If you want. Or later if—"

"Now's good," Crosby interrupted. "I'll bring some wine."

"Okay."

"Okay."

He hung up, put the laundry in the dryer, and brushed his teeth. He had a man coming over.

# Chapter Fourteen

---

@sawyerscovedaily Is it a coincidence the next episode airs on New Year's Day? I think technically it'll drop at midnight on New Year's Eve and we can all ring in the new year Sawyer's Cove style. #sawyerscove #happynewyear

---

*New Year's Eve*

TREVOR

So how's it going with Darren? I haven't heard from you all week, so I figure it's going well.

CROSBY

It's good.

Oh, you gotta give me more than that.

It's really good.

We've been spending a lot of time together.

New Year's Eve plans?

We're going to Ariel's for game night.

Oh, so fun!! Take pictures so I can live vicariously through you and your famous friends, please?

I will try to remember to take a picture. What are you doing for New Year's?

Actually, I do have plans. A friend from high school is back home for the holidays and he's throwing a little shindig.

Have fun. I gotta go. Audition.

You will slay. Later.

∾

DARREN

Call me when you're done.

Or text. Whatever.

Break a leg.

CROSBY

I think you're more nervous than I am.

I think I am too. But you're going to
smash it.

Thanks.

You think they'll tell you if you got it
right away?

No clue.

Either way, I'll give you a BJ.

BJ? Are you fourteen?

I'm trying to be discreet. What if our
texts get hacked?

Then people will know how sappy
you are.

And that you give me blow jobs.
Everyone knows what BJ stands for.

Fine. Maybe I won't give you one then.

We have to go to Ariel's tonight,
anyway.

She has a bathroom.

Gross. You aren't blowing me in our
friend's bathroom.

Why not? It would probably be the
highlight of her year, sadly.

Gotta go. The other actor's here.

CROSBY

Done.

DARREN

And???????

Where are you? Should I come over?

Getting snacks. Ariel called me in a
panic about goat cheese.

"Hey, figured it was easier to call."

"Tell me everything. I'm on line to check out."

Crosby let out a pent-up breath at Darren's words. He'd just spent a nerve-wracking two hours trying to land the *Dessert First* role, and hearing his boyfriend's voice instantly grounded him.

"The guy they brought in for Hank was really good. Remy Jackson—I think he was in an indie sci-fi movie last year?"

"Oh, yeah. He's cute. Gay?"

"Not sure. But he played gay really well."

"What about you? Did they buy your gay schtick?"

"Fuck you," Crosby said without heat. He had, in fact, casually mentioned to the director he was gay. Bruce had raised his eyebrows half an inch, as if it was news to him, but he didn't think it hurt his chances.

"Soon, I hope," Darren returned.

Crosby almost tripped over a nonexistent crack in the sidewalk on 34^th Street. They hadn't fucked yet. They'd both been trying to stick to the plan—one step at a time, even when all he wanted to do sometimes was rush headlong into the deep end and drag Darren along with him.

He valiantly tried to keep his mind on the subject at hand and not imagine the first possible scenario in which they could take that particular step.

"Anyway, yes, they must have bought it, because they offered me the part."

"Of course they did." Darren sounded as if he'd been in complete certainty about the outcome of the audition. "Congratulations, Crosby."

"Thanks." It was always a good feeling to get a "yes" when so much of being an actor was hearing "no." "Rehearsals start in about a month. I checked with my agent, and the official offer already came through."

"They really want you," Darren said, pride in his voice. "I know the feeling."

Crosby's cheeks hurt with the size of the grin on his face. He wasn't sure how life could get much better. He'd been offered the part for a role he really, really wanted, and he had a supportive boyfriend who couldn't wait to congratulate him in person. He checked his watch.

"I'm going to go home and change. Should I meet you at Ariel's?"

"Yeah. This line is wild. Everyone in New York except you is in this Zabar's. I'll head over from here."

"See you there."

He took a moment to send a Happy New Year's text to his parents, who were still in London. He sent one to Trevor to tell him the audition went well. He didn't tell him he got the part because, while Trevor was a good kid, you couldn't be too careful with information leaks these days, and the producers had said they were waiting to make a formal casting announcement until after the new year.

He got to his apartment. He'd spent very little time there this week. Somehow, he and Darren had ended up spending most nights at Darren's place, small and cluttered as it was. It was cozy, though, and had personality. He hadn't been in the building very long and hadn't yet put his stamp on the place. All the same, Darren's place was probably too small for both of them, long-term. He wondered if they would be one of those couples who kept their own places, or if they'd maybe want to choose an apartment to move into together some day. If they ended up with a kid down the road, cohabiting definitely made more sense—

He stopped himself as he buttoned up a fresh shirt. This one was stark black, and he had a metallic gold tie to add. It had only been a week since they'd spent their first night together in Misty Harbor. Way too soon to be thinking about moving in together or kids, for goodness' sake.

Crosby took a deep breath, willing himself to believe they had time for all of that in the future. All he had to worry about tonight was showing his boyfriend a good time. They were going to Ariel's party, which she promised would be close friends only. Knowing their friends, that didn't help.

He and Darren hadn't gone public yet. Trevor and Ariel knew, and that was it. But it was bound to come out, eventually. He wasn't worried about the press. He'd been through it all, and overall he'd been lucky to keep his private life private. He was more worried about the way this might affect the dynamic of the *Sawyer's Cove* cast, which was already borderline codependent.

He finished dressing, grabbed the bottle of wine he'd promised to bring, put on his coat, and went to face the music.

Ariel lived on the top floor of a short building in the West Village, with lots of windows and a big open kitchen blending into the living room. Her living room was the perfect game playing space, with a long wooden table and straight-backed chairs clustered around. She had a lavishly appointed bar cart set up on one side, and another table absolutely covered with food on the other. Darren was arguing with her when Crosby arrived.

"Why did I risk my sanity going to Zabar's on New Year's Eve when you have enough food here to feed the entire block?"

"Because I needed goat cheese, and oh, those olives are my favorite. Hand them over," Ariel said, stealing the shopping bag out of Darren's hand. "Crosby, hey!" She gave him a violent peck on the cheek. "You have the sweetest boyfriend."

"I know," Crosby said, unable to stop himself from twinkling at said boyfriend, who still looked annoyed. "You're beautiful, Ariel." His host wore a formfitting black dress, black boots, and chunky gold jewelry at her wrists and ears.

"Thank you, you look...glam," she said tactfully, tweaking his gold tie. "But at least you match me. Your boy didn't get the memo to dress up."

"This is dressed up for me," Darren protested. "You didn't say I had to wear a tie."

"You're beautiful, too," Crosby teased. Darren was wearing dark jeans and sneakers and a black sweater. He was freshly shaven and smelled good enough to eat. Crosby had to stop himself from pulling him in and palming his ass in those jeans, but PDA wasn't something they'd worked their way up to either.

"Thanks, honey." Darren fluttered his eyelashes back, and they grinned at each other. Where did the fake flirting stop, and the real flirting begin? The line was pretty thin. Crosby couldn't seem to care.

Ariel made a gagging noise. "I take it back. I thought you would be adorable together, but it turns out you're just disgustingly cute. I'm both incredibly jealous and want to throw up a little."

"You're welcome," Darren said smugly.

"Anytime," Crosby added. "So, we're the first ones here?"

"I told you two to come an hour earlier than

everyone else, and you only came half an hour late, so technically you're early."

"Devious."

"I know you, that's all."

They helped themselves to drinks, and Darren piled a plate with food. "You must be hungry," he said, putting the plate in Crosby's hands.

"This is for me?"

"Yeah. Sorry?" Darren looked uncertain.

"No, it's great. Thanks." He was starving. He'd been too nervous to eat before the audition, and then too elated to eat afterward. But now, with the adrenaline fading, the warmth of Ariel's radiators, and Darren smiling at him like he couldn't believe his luck to be there with him, he was ravenous. The cheese and crackers and hummus were the best things he'd ever eaten. The wine he'd brought tasted like nectar of the gods. Was this what being happy did to the world? Added a sheen of deliciousness, making life that much shinier?

Crosby had always had a weakness for a bit of shine.

A few minutes later, Ariel opened the door to the next guests.

"We can't stay long," Selena said by way of greeting.

The head writer and showrunner of the *Sawyer's Cove* reboot was dressed for the cold weather in a ruby red wool coat with a dazzling scarlet dress underneath. Her ears winked with giant diamond studs, but her real accessory was Warner Mathis, her boyfriend. They'd met while Selena was in Misty Harbor to produce the first season of the show, and they'd stayed together once the shoot was over.

The entire cast had spent Christmas Day watching the first episode of the reboot at Warner's house in Misty Harbor, which was where Crosby met him only a week ago, the day he'd shared Darren's room at the Misty Harbor Inn because of a snowstorm, and his life had changed forever.

"Why can't you stay?" Ariel pouted. "We have tons of fun games planned."

"My friend's throwing a big bash, and I promised we'd come," Warner said, grimacing apologetically.

Crosby empathized. It wasn't appealing to let Ariel Tulip down.

"Yeah, I'm going to meet all his New York friends," Selena said, sounding slightly apprehensive.

"They're going to love you," Warner said, his face transforming as he looked at Selena. Love softened his normally grim expression and made him appear ten years younger. "Believe me, they're going to think you're way better than I deserve."

"Oh, stop." Selena laughed. "I hope *I* like *them*," she said, regaining her usual confidence.

Warner chuckled. "If you don't, we'll leave early and—"

Selena batted her eyelashes at him suggestively. "And?"

Warner glanced around their audience. Ariel beamed. Darren leered charmingly. Crosby winked at

Warner. "And we'll toast on our own," he finished self-consciously.

Selena let out a peal of throaty laughter. "Sounds like a plan." Then she waved to Darren and Crosby. "Hey, glad to see you both so soon after Christmas."

Darren had drifted to Crosby's side. "Nice to see you, too," he said. Crosby knew he was thinking about the possibility of directing next season, but now was not the time for business.

"I was worried about you both in the storm the other day," she went on. "Did it give you any problems?"

"We had to stay at the inn for a couple of days," Darren said, glancing at Crosby conspiratorially. "But we put the time to good use."

Crosby coughed. They hadn't discussed telling people, but it wasn't like it was going to stay a secret. On the other hand, it had only been a week. On the other, other hand, he didn't want to pretend like he and Darren were just friends all night. He coughed again, his throat dry.

Selena furrowed her brow. "You need some water?"

"No, I—" He glanced at Darren. How were they going to do this? He lifted his eyebrows, and Darren waggled his back unhelpfully. He took a deep breath. "Uh, by the way—"

A knock on the door halted his words.

"Who else is coming? Jay and Cami?" Selena asked.

Ariel spoke on her way to the door. "No, they're staying in Misty Harbor. He gave his bar manager a vacation, so he's sticking close to The Cove. And Mimi and

Nash are there, too. But I do have other friends besides our *Sawyer's Cove* clique, you know."

She opened the door and squealed when she saw the woman standing there. "Kate!"

There was an equally loud squeal, and then another tall, buxom redhead appeared, throwing her arms around their hostess. "Hey, you. You remember Oliver, right?"

A dark-haired, dark-eyed man followed the redhead in. Crosby took a close look at the woman—Kate? She was really familiar.

"Everyone, this is Kate Treanor and Oliver Mercier. They're visiting us from Los Angeles. Where is the baby?"

"Maverick is with my parents," Oliver said smoothly. "We thought about bringing him, but my mother would have been devastated to have her babysitting privileges revoked. We got in yesterday, and I'm pretty sure she hasn't put him down except for naps."

"I'm going to want to see him, too," Ariel cooed. "I can't believe he's going to be two tomorrow."

"I know, hardly a baby anymore," Kate said. "But let me say hi to everyone else before I pull out my phone and show you a billion photos."

"Kate, meet Warner Mathis," Ariel said, "and I don't know if you know Selena Echeveria."

"No, but I'm a huge fan." Kate smiled, and Crosby finally placed her.

"You were on *Sawyer's Cove*," he said. "One of the

final episodes, wasn't it? I'm Crosby," he said, feeling foolish since she obviously knew who he was.

She smiled in recognition. "Hi, Crosby."

"Oh, yeah," Darren said. "I remember you. You played Will's cousin. I'm Darren, by the way."

Kate laughed. "Hi, Darren. Wow, you two have great memories. My guest spot on *Sawyer's Cove* was the highlight of a brief acting career. That's where I met Ariel, and when she and I ran into each other on another show a few months later, we got to be friends."

"I impose on her when I have to go to L.A.," Ariel said, "and she and Oliver have been more than gracious. My advice—make friends with someone who owns a restaurant, and you'll never go hungry."

"You're not acting anymore?" Crosby remembered her clearly now. She looked the same as thirteen years ago, a little curvier, but she fairly glowed.

"I'm a podcast producer."

Crosby perked up. "I'm a big podcast listener. Any shows I might have heard?"

"*Brew O'Clock* is my most popular pod. We just launched another food-oriented show—that's Oliver's influence. He owns Mercy restaurant and a couple of other places." She tipped her head toward Oliver, who was being shown the buffet by Ariel. Crosby understood her goat cheese panic a little better now.

"I love *Brew O'Clock*." Crosby had a few episodes queued up to listen to when he had a minute. "I never recognized your name in the credits, I'm sorry. But that's so cool."

"Thanks." She smiled. "And you guys must be so proud of the show's spectacular debut. I watched the first two episodes. Can't wait for the next one—it comes out tomorrow, I think."

"I almost forgot," Crosby said. "It's been a whirlwind of a week."

Darren laughed. "The whirlwindiest."

They looked at each other and smiled. Oh goodness, they were being transparent, but he couldn't manage to care.

"Want a drink?" Darren asked Kate, breaking eye contact with Crosby.

"I think I'm being delivered one, thanks," she said, nodding as Oliver approached with a glass of wine.

"How about you? Refill?" Darren asked him.

Crosby drained the last sip in his glass simply for the novelty of having an attractive man bring him a fresh one. He tracked Darren crossing the room, belatedly realizing Kate and Oliver were watching him, amused.

"So, what brings you to New York?" he asked, hoping he wasn't blushing.

"We're visiting my folks and viewing some properties," Oliver said.

"Residential or commercial?"

"Residential. For now. We might be one of those annoying bicoastal families, at least until Mav gets old enough for school," Oliver said. "My parents are uptown, and if all goes well, I'll be opening a restaurant here in the city in the next year or so. It would be nicer to have our own place if we're going to be traveling back and forth."

They talked about the neighborhoods they were interested in, and the pros of living in Los Angeles versus New York. Crosby liked Los Angeles in small doses, but he'd never want to live there full time.

"Same," Darren said. "I'm a New Yorker, born and bred. Not sure I could really live anywhere else."

"We're already bicoastal ourselves," Selena added. "But Misty Harbor isn't as easy to get to as New York."

"What is it about Misty Harbor?" Kate asked. "Ariel told me Camille Corsair and Jay Orlando are ensconced up there, too. I remember it being charming, but what's the big deal?"

Warner, unexpectedly, spoke up. "It's beautiful, but it's also real. I love Los Angeles, but Misty Harbor grows on a person. It's small enough to feel homey and big enough to disappear for a while, if you need to."

Selena looked up at him. "And there's not much to do besides work when you're on a show. We'll be back there later next year for season two."

"Have we set a date for the filming?" Crosby asked.

"Why? Don't tell me you're busy?" Selena said, alarmed.

"He booked the lead in the next Bruce Taylor movie," Darren said proudly.

Selena's eyes darted between the two of them, her eyes narrowing at how they were standing less than a foot apart. "Congratulations, Crosby," she said, her voice warm but her eyes hard.

"It wraps in March," Crosby said, "and after that, my schedule is open."

"Oh, good." Selena sounded relieved. "We probably won't start until summer at the earliest." To Darren, she said, "And I haven't forgotten about you directing, believe me. You should be getting a call from someone at the studio after the new year to talk about your availability."

Darren grinned. "Fantastic."

"Enough talking about work," Ariel said, "though I am excited for you, Crosby. We're here to play some games."

"We're going to have to run," Selena said. "But I'm sure I'll talk to all of you soon. Kate, really great to meet you. I loved your episode of the old show."

"Thanks. Wow. I love, like, everything you've ever done, so that's amazing," Kate said, laughing merrily.

Warner and Selena said their goodbyes. Selena gave Crosby a sharp stare as she put her red coat back on.

"Hang on," he said to Darren, and followed Selena to the door.

"Is there something you want to know?" She was his boss. He didn't want her to be thinking the worst.

"It's none of my business," she said, glancing subtly in Darren's direction.

"It's okay. You might as well know. Darren and I are —" He stopped, not exactly sure what the right word to use was.

"Together," came Darren's voice from a few feet away.

Crosby looked behind him. Darren gave him a small smile and a nod. He turned back to Selena. "Yeah. So. FYI."

She pressed her lips together, then said, "Okay, good to know. Sorry if I'm being weird, it's just, well. Everyone knows you guys don't get along. So I'm a little lost."

"Yeah, about that." Crosby was struck again by how difficult he'd made everyone's lives for the past fifteen years. He wondered if he'd ever live it down. He decided if he had Darren at the end of the day, it didn't matter.

"Turns out we were sublimating our mutual attraction for each other by being antagonistic," Darren said, with a saucy glint in his eye.

Crosby stared at him. "Is that what we were doing?"

"I'm pretty sure that's what *you* were doing," Darren said. "I'm still playing catch up."

Crosby's shoulders rose, his defenses activated by Darren's casually devastating statement. He knew Darren didn't mean anything by it, but he couldn't help his instinct to deflect and deny and turn the tables. He tried to smile; he was pretty sure the effort resembled a sick cat baring its teeth.

But then Darren slipped his hand into Crosby's and Crosby realized none of it mattered—not the past, not the future. They were together, right now, and he didn't care what anybody else thought about it. Not Selena, not the fans, not his parents, though they'd probably find Darren delightful.

"You're right," he said, with eyes for Darren alone. "Hurry up and catch me, won't you?"

"Working on it," Darren said. He squeezed Crosby's hand, and Crosby knew everything was going to be okay.

Selena and Warner left, all smiles as Ariel called, "Come on, you guys, we're starting."

Darren looked at Crosby. "So, you wanna play a game?"

He planted a kiss on his boyfriend's mouth. Darren opened up for him easily, kissing him back with a familiarity that made Crosby's heart clench with gratitude for being given a chance to be with someone who made him so damn happy.

"Yeah, let's go play."

# Chapter Fifteen



*Eight months later*

Crosby opened his eyes and looked at his phone. Three whole minutes before his alarm. Sighing, he disabled the alarm and sat up, glancing at the empty spot in the king bed next to him. He noted the light under the adjoining bathroom door, heard the water in the sink turn on, then off. He stretched and got out of bed, padding over to the bathroom door. He tapped, and the door swung open to reveal a fully dressed Darren, freshly shaved and smelling like pine-scented moisturizer.

"You're up already?"

"Call at seven," Darren said. "Gotta get to work, babe." He tried to move around Crosby but was stopped by Crosby's hand on his chest.

"Hey, you're not nervous, are you?"

"It's my first day on set, of course I'm nervous," he said, with a wry smile.

"It's going to be amazing. You're an amazing director."

"True," Darren said, without conviction.

"Besides, you have your favorite actor on set today," Crosby said, wrapping his hands around Darren's waist and squeezing lightly.

"Oh, right, Nash is in some of the scenes today," Darren said slyly.

Crosby squeezed harder. "Not who I meant."

"Trevor, too. He's doing a fabulous job, by the way."

Trevor had auditioned during the now-traditional *Sawyer's Cove* open casting call, and according to Selena and Cami, he'd nailed it. He was cast as a record store clerk for a single episode guest spot, but after seeing the dailies, Selena had written his character into a couple more episodes this season. He was still working at the Bakeshop, but Crosby could tell the big city was calling his friend, and he couldn't be prouder. He'd already talked to his agent about meeting with Trevor once this season was wrapped.

Crosby tightened his hold on his boyfriend, and Darren let out an exaggerated oof. "I meant me, jerk."

"Oh, *you.*" Darren laughed and wrapped his arms around Crosby in return. "As excited as I am about directing you making out with Ariel, it's not the part I'm worried about. You guys are pros. You are off script, right?"

Crosby arched a single eyebrow. "What do you think?"

"Of course you are. You know you're telling her you love her today, right? Nervous? It's a pretty big scene."

"Spencer is telling Lily he loves her. Me and Ariel have nothing to do with it," Crosby said, aiming for nonchalance.

"So you're nervous," Darren concluded.

"A little." He stuck his tongue out. They'd been together for over eight months, and every day he'd grown fonder of the man he'd never thought would look his way. Still, that didn't mean he wasn't annoying as hell on some days.

Crosby knew Darren was deflecting his own nerves about directing his first *Sawyer's Cove* episode, and he was honestly happy to help now that the shoe was on the other foot.

Darren had held his hand—literally and metaphori- cally—through the difficult but rewarding shoot for *Dessert First*, then helped him deal with the frankly disproportionate, in Crosby's eyes anyway, media attention the revelation of their relationship caused in the press. Apparently, he wasn't as out as he thought he was, and when he and Darren started showing up at Broadway shows and New York restaurants together, especially in the wake of the smashing success of the *Sawyer's Cove* reboot, it had been all over social media for what seemed like months.

Things had calmed down since the summer, or maybe Crosby had been too busy to worry about what strangers on the Internet were saying. Darren had been working nonstop, too. He'd guest directed steadily all winter and spring, then found out Noah was being brought back as a series regular for the second season of *Sawyer's Cove*.

Crosby had already had to deal with Darren and Nash shooting Noah and Will's sex scene a couple of episodes ago. Being a direct-to-streaming show meant they could show a little more than the old days on the network. Obviously, he hadn't been on set the day of shooting, but he and Darren had talked about what the director of the episode had in mind. The weirdness of imagining his boyfriend and one of his closest colleagues and friends pretending to make love aside, Crosby was sure it was going to be a fan-favorite episode.

"You know how you're going to play it? The love confession, I mean?" Darren asked as he put on the designer watch Crosby had given him for his birthday a couple of months ago—a plain black face punctuated with a single diamond stud positioned over the 12.

"Are you asking as my director or my boyfriend?"

Darren pretended to think. "Both."

"Yeah, I think I do." He actually was a little nervous about the scene. Sawyer and Lily had been through a lot of ups and downs, including in this season alone, and Sawyer's never told her he loves her before. It was clearly going to be a pivotal moment for the entire arc of the show. "But I might try a few different things," he said, knowing Darren would be in director mode later.

"You could always draw on life experience," Darren said, still playful.

"What do you mean?" Crosby said innocently.

Darren looked at his mouth and up again. "Remember when you told your favorite director you loved him?"

It was Crosby's turn to pretend to think. "I don't think I ever told Martin Scorsese I loved him."

Darren groaned theatrically. "Okay, how about when you told me?"

"Oh, that. I do remember that." Crosby had known he was in love with Darren from practically the beginning of their relationship, but he'd also known it would have been crazy to say it out loud before they'd been dating for some reasonable length of time. They hit the two-week mark. Then one month. They spent nearly every night together, alternating between their apartments. Filming began on *Dessert First,* and then Darren had a directing gig in Toronto, and they were apart for ten days, talking on the phone every night.

The night he got back, Crosby had been vibrating

like a puppy in the lobby of Darren's apartment build-ing, waiting for the car service to arrive from the airport. They'd given each other messy hand jobs on the couch in Darren's living room, then eaten takeout Thai and ended up in bed, Darren fucking Crosby for only the second time since they started dating.

Darren preferred to bottom, which Crosby found out the first time they fucked, on New Year's Day. Crosby had been all set to prep himself, but Darren had asked him to top, and they'd done it that way nearly every time since. Crosby liked both, and there was nothing sexier than Darren breathily asking him to fuck him, as if he didn't get Crosby's dick in him right that second, the world might end.

But that night, after Thai food and sex, Crosby had felt the words pressing against his chest, the *I love you* practically stamped on his forehead, threatening to stutter out of him every time he opened his mouth. He kept biting down the words. A month and a half was too soon, he berated himself. Darren seemed to be into him, and he wasn't going to jeopardize the good thing they had going by scaring him off with feelings talk.

They had cleaned themselves up and were getting ready to go to sleep in Darren's bed when Darren said casually, "I realized something on my trip."

"Oh, yeah?" Crosby thought he was going to say something like "Toronto weather sucks" or "We should always fly first-class."

But Darren said, "I love you."

"You what?" Crosby was stunned. Had Darren just beaten him to the "I love you" punch?

"I love you?" A question this time.

Crosby decided he didn't care if he'd been shown up by his boyfriend. Darren loved him. He'd been waiting for his boyfriend to catch up, and he finally had. "I love you, too."

"Oh." Darren looked relieved. "Good."

"You didn't know?" Crosby was an actor, but he wasn't that good.

"I...hoped," Darren said, and it was so sweet and so everything Crosby had ever wanted, he felt like he might cry.

They'd said "I love you" approximately one thousand times since, but it hadn't gotten old yet. Crosby was pretty sure it never would.

In their room at the Misty Harbor Inn, getting ready to spend the day doing work they enjoyed, Darren at the helm of the episode, Crosby playing the character that had made his career, for an audience that had been resoundingly supportive of their relationship once it had been made public knowledge, Crosby knew saying "I love you" to Lily was a big deal. But none of it meant as much without Darren to come home to at the end of the day.

For all he had been worried about getting into a relationship with a co-worker, it turned out to make things even better on set. He and Darren were finally slated to share some one-on-one scenes later in the season, and he couldn't wait to act with the man he loved.

"Hey," Darren said, mischief in his eyes, "I dare you to make Ariel screw up the first take."

"Hell, no," Crosby said. "You want Selena to fire us both?"

"She wouldn't fire me, she loves me," Darren said.

"Everyone loves you," Crosby complained. It was still as true as ever.

"Including you," Darren said happily.

"Especially me."

# Epilogue

*Ten months later*

Ariel Tulip was starving.

She'd driven to Misty Harbor from New York in one straight shot. It had taken her longer to get out of the city than she'd planned, and her apartment just off Misty Harbor's Main Street had an empty refrigerator. She hadn't been there since Harbor Fest, over a month ago, and she hadn't hit the market to stock up yet. Her pantry held the staples—olives, crackers, and champagne—but she craved something hot and greasy.

Luckily, her apartment was a block from Melba's, the retro fifties diner. She parked, left her bags in the car, and made a beeline for the restaurant. The lunch rush was over, and the early dinner crowd hadn't started yet. In fact, there were only a half dozen customers in the place, including a familiar man sitting at the counter with a cup of coffee and an open laptop in front of him.

"Hey, Loretta," Ariel greeted the server who materialized with a menu.

"Hi, sweetie," Loretta said laconically. "Sit anywhere."

Ariel nodded. She usually asked for a window booth if one was free, but today she went to the counter. "Fancy meeting you here."

Ryan Saylor, the creator of *Sawyer's Cove*, the man who'd hired sixteen-year-old Ariel to play Lily Fine, changing her life with her first big break, looked away from his computer and into her eyes.

The look in his gray-green-brown irises shifted from distracted and wary to surprised, then warm.

"Ariel, hi," he said, swiveling the high-backed stool so he could half stand up and hug her lightly in greeting.

She hugged him back, then dropped onto the stool next to him and surveyed him. He wore brown corduroy pants, and a green plaid shirt under a tweed jacket complete with elbow patch, like an English professor from 1985. The jacket's left arm had been removed and tailored so it ended at the shoulder, due to his limb difference. Ryan had been born without a left arm.

She hadn't seen him in person in years, and there were new fine lines around his eyes. His chestnut brown hair was shorter than when he'd been the precocious twenty-five-year-old in charge of his own TV show, but it still curled around his ears and nearly brushed the collar of his jacket.

"So, what are you doing in my neck of the woods?" Ariel asked.

"Oh, is this your neighborhood? I thought you lived in the West Village."

"When I'm not in Misty Harbor," Ariel agreed. "As of five minutes ago, I live right around the corner until we wrap."

"Still? Didn't you live somewhere around here back in the day?"

Ariel was surprised he remembered. "I did, and I do. In the very same apartment, actually. The first season of the reboot, I made inquiries, but someone else was renting it, so I stayed at the inn. But when the last tenants moved out, the landlord offered it to me. I've been here off and on for over a year now. I like having my own space, and it's handy for Harbor Fest and Cove Con."

"With Jay and Cami and Nash all settled here, it really feels like Misty Harbor is your second home."

"I'm a city girl at heart," Ariel reminded him, "but it's nice to get away from Manhattan sometimes, too. Misty Harbor is a regular Cloudy Cove."

"So I'm learning," Ryan said.

"When did you arrive? Wait." Ariel flagged down Loretta and ordered a grilled cheese with tomato and a chocolate banana milkshake. "You want anything else?"

"No, I ate, thanks," Ryan said. He glanced at his computer screen, which had gone dark.

"Oh, I'm keeping you from your work." She'd been so excited to see a friendly face that it hadn't occurred to her he might not want her company. Story of her life. She went on being her effusive, emotional self, and usually far too late picked up on the clues that she was too much for some people. Most people, actually.

"It's okay," he said quickly. "Just banging my head against some spreadsheets. Selena left everything in great shape, but I already feel behind. I'm better at words than numbers."

Ariel had been as shocked as anyone when, a couple of months ago, showrunner Selena Echeveria had announced she was turning over the reins of the third and final season of the *Sawyer's Cove* reboot to Ryan, the original creator. Selena had been given a green light to turn her boyfriend Warner Mathis's bestselling mystery novel *Gunsmoke* into a limited series. But studio backing depended on casting one of Hollywood's biggest stars in the role of Jake Wilton, the private detective hero, and the star in question's availability had overlapped with the *Sawyer's Cove* shoot, so she'd had no choice but to step away. Lucky for all of them, Ryan had agreed to take her place.

She already missed Selena and her steady, no-nonsense hand, but none of the *Sawyer's Cove* family had wanted her to lose out on this opportunity. Plus, it was exciting to have Ryan come back to the show. Ariel was determined that the third and final season was going to be amazing for the cast and crew. They'd been given a gift with this reboot. It had been a chance to renew old friendships, for new relationships to blossom, and for fans to fall in love with the show all over again. It was only when she thought about the end of the shoot, about three months away, that she, typically for her, got weepy.

Once the season was over, the core group of actors wouldn't have any reason to get together with the same regularity they had for the past three years. She was going to miss the camaraderie. On top of which, she wasn't sure which direction she should try to take her career in. Everyone else had their lane, seemed to be cruising along in it, while she was barely keeping up.

It also didn't help that everyone was oh-so-happily paired up. Ryan had only dealt with one on-set romance the first go-round. As she bit gratefully into her sandwich, she filled him in on the rest of the gossip.

"So you know about Jay and Cami, obviously." Their rekindled romance had been all over social media, fanning the flames of excitement for the reboot in the process. "But how up are you on the rest of the *Sawyer's Cove* news?"

Ryan cringed. "Do I really need to know? Surely everyone keeps things professional."

"Sure, we're all pros. But you need to know the basics. Want a quick primer?"

"Will there be a test?"

"Oh, definitely," Ariel said with a wink. "And I'm a very hard grader."

"Then I better pay attention," he said, closing his computer and turning toward her.

She shifted in her seat, suddenly self-conscious. She was used to an audience, but not an audience of one.

Ryan was giving her his full attention, and it felt nice—but unsettling.

He'd always intimidated her—he was so smart, so much older than her, more worldly and experienced.

Over a decade later, the age difference didn't strike her as that big a deal anymore. He was what—forty-one? Forty-two? But it was hard not to feel a little nervous around him all the same. He was essentially her boss, even if he was the new kid in town.

"Well, Nash is with Jay's sister, Mimi, who's the head of the town library. They have this awesome old Victorian house. They did a bunch of work to it and turned the basement into a recording studio for Nash, and the first floor has this library out of a fairy tale, I swear. They're having a barbecue this weekend, if you didn't already hear, so you can see it for yourself."

Ryan's face rippled, but she couldn't read his reaction, so she plowed on. "And of course, Crosby and Darren are together. I'm assuming Darren will be around a fair bit, between directing and things going well with Noah and Will *finally* after all the drama last season. Please don't tell me you're going to break them up, because I might have to hurt you."

"You and every other fangirl," Ryan said, holding his hand up defensively. "Don't worry. Will and Noah will get their happily ever after."

"Excellent. Which means we'll be seeing a lot of Darren, and Crosby will be happy. They're nauseatingly in love."

"And what about you?" Ryan asked.

Ariel took a long pull on her milkshake while he stared at her steadily. "What about me?"

"Who's your significant other? A local hero or a New Yorker?"

Ariel squinted at him, but Ryan didn't appear to be joking. She ignored the stab of sadness his words invoked and decided to keep things as airy as the meringue on the pie in the refrigerated case behind the counter. "Alas, I'm but a poor unattached female."

Ryan's brow creased, as if he didn't understand the concept.

"Somehow I've managed to escape the love curse that seems to affect everyone else when they get inside Misty Harbor's city limits," she went on gaily. "What about you?"

Ryan took a second to respond. "I'm single, too. Divorced."

Ariel had heard about his divorce. She'd never met his wife, but they'd been married for a while. She wondered what had happened.

"We could start a club," she said. "Sawyer's Cove Singles."

Ryan stroked his chin. "Or we could pair up and appease the Misty Harbor love gods before anything terrible befalls the town."

She grinned at his over-the-top suggestion. "Oh yes, we could make ourselves tributes by dating each other. Great idea."

Ryan's cheeks colored at her acquiescence. "No, I

wouldn't put you through that. I'm hopeless at dating. I think I'll just enter my crotchety-old-man phase early."

"Nonsense." Ryan might dress like an aging professor, but he was far from elderly. His clean-shaven face had small lines that made him look distinguished, while his body was as lean as ever. Ariel didn't know what kind of exercise he did to keep fit, but whatever he did, it was working. "I may not be great at dating myself, but I am an amazing wing-woman."

Ryan laughed. "Oh, I don't doubt it."

"I could get you a date to the barbecue by tomorrow," she persisted, feeling as if she had something to prove, even though he wasn't challenging her.

"The barbecue. Nash mentioned it, but I don't know that I should go."

"Why not? Everyone will be so excited to see you."

"I have a pile of work. And you'll have more fun without me."

"What are you talking about?" She was genuinely mystified.

"Just that you're all so close. It's awesome, but I'm like the stuffy dad or the weird uncle."

"Is that how you see yourself? You gave us our livelihoods. You created *Sawyer's Cove*."

"A million years ago. I'm a fossil. Anyway, I have so much work to do I can't—"

"You can and you will, Ryan Saylor," Ariel declared. "I expect to see you at that barbecue, and I'll bring someone nice for you. Even if you just make a friend, you could always use another friend, couldn't you?"

"I suppose." He looked at her thoughtfully. "Does anyone ever say no to you?"

She laughed. "Only all the time. But I'm glad my powers of persuasion work on you, at least."

"You make it easy to say yes."

"Really?" The comment pleased her. She always worked hard to make things happen, in her life, in her career. It was nice to feel a sense of ease around someone for a change.

"And what about you?"

She sucked noisily on the dregs of her milkshake, then peered into the empty glass, but there was no hidden compartment filled with more at the bottom. "What do you mean?"

"Am I supposed to bring a guy for you? Like a *When Harry Met Sally* thing?"

Delighted as she was by him referencing one of her favorite movies of all time, she shook her head vehemently. "Absolutely not. I don't think you'll be able to find my soulmate in forty-eight hours when I haven't found him in thirty-three years."

"Your soulmate?" His brow furrowed. "I was thinking more like a nice, regular Misty Harbor resident."

"I already know I'm not going to find my soulmate in Misty Harbor," she said. "I've spent so much time here in the last couple of years, I can't imagine I wouldn't have met him already."

"Sorry, but what's with the soulmate obsession?"

"Isn't that the dream—to find the person who completes you? Your other half?"

"Dream?" He scoffed. "It's a fantasy, Ariel, take it from me."

"This from the man who wrote all those beautiful monologues for Sawyer about looking for his soulmate?"

He grimaced. "I was young and romantic. And Sawyer never found his soulmate, remember?"

She bristled. Sawyer had been with Lily Fine for most of season two of the reboot, and she was beginning to think they had been endgame this entire time.

"Nope, uh-uh, you aren't allowed to take this from me. I need something to justify being pathetically alone while all my friends find the loves of their lives in this one-horse town. No offense, Loretta," Ariel said to the server who was picking up her empty plate.

"None taken, hon. Want dessert?"

"The milkshake was enough for me. Just the check."

Loretta slid a piece of paper onto the counter and shuffled away.

Ariel dug out her wallet and removed some cash. "I will see you at the barbecue. Oh, this is going to be such a bittersweet season. I'm sad already." She sniffed, then brightened. "But finding you a girlfriend, despite you no longer being young and romantic, is a worthy challenge. See you soon, boss."

Ryan chuckled, but when she didn't laugh, he stopped her before she left. "Wait, Ariel—if you're serious about the date thing, I have one rule. No actresses."

"No actresses?" She frowned. "What's wrong with actresses?"

His expression turned sheepish, as if he'd belatedly remembered what she did for a living. "Sorry, it's just a thing I've had since I first got to Hollywood. I don't date actresses."

"No actresses," she said crisply. Well, whatever. It wasn't like she was going to set him up with anyone from the cast. That would be unprofessional.

"No offense," he said weakly.

She channeled her inner Loretta. "None taken, hon." Then she swept out of the diner with all the haughtiness she could muster.

No actresses, indeed.

Thank you so much for taking a chance on Crosby and Darren's story!
Scan the code to download the free Sawyer's Cove: The Reboot prequel story, *Kate's Take*, and get to know Ryan and Ariel back when they were making the original Sawyer's Cove!

xoxo,
Libby

# Enjoy an excerpt from Take Two, the first book in the Sawyer's Cove: The Reboot series

JULES: Okay, we're doing this. Are we doing this?

ERIKA: Hey, I bought this fancy microphone with my birthday money. We're doing this.

JULES: All right, then, let's go. Welcome to the first episode of *The Sawyer's Cove Rewatch Project* podcast. Jesus, that's a mouthful.

ERIKA: That's what Lily Fine said. Bah-dum-ch!

JULES: Wow, are we getting into the Lily-Fine-is-a-slut jokes already? Do we need to start some kind of counter?

ERIKA: Sorry, sorry. I'll be good. For those of you who don't know, *Sawyer's Cove* was a television show that ran for three beautiful, shamefully short seasons before it was canceled by evil television executives.

JULES: A lot of people became fans after it went to streaming, but Erika and I actually watched it live, being in the target audience of teenage girls at the time. But its cancellation broke my heart, so I left it behind and moved on to different pursuits. Erika, meanwhile—

Erika: I never stopped. I had all the DVDs, the sound-track, the Parker Wild posters, the whole shebang.

Jules: I haven't seen the show in over a decade, so we're both rewatching from the beginning.

Erika: Yeah, and then we talk about it and all you other *Cove* freaks can get your nostalgia fix. So, buckle up for drama, sex, tears, laughs, bad hair, and good chemistry. Let's do this.


From *The Sawyer's Cove Rewatch Project Podcast: Pilot*


Cami had expected Misty Harbor to be exactly the same. It lived in her memory as a static image, the quaint downtown with its brick two-story buildings frozen behind snow globe glass.

She remembered the narrow two-lane Main Street, anchored at one end by the Victorian-era mansion-turned-inn and at the other by the rocky beach and Atlantic Ocean, as it had been the last time she saw it, the final day of shooting *Sawyer's Cove*. Her father had rushed her to the airport right after wrapping so she could audition for a Spielberg movie she didn't get.

There had been a wrap party, eventually, out in L.A. She'd seen all her castmates again, when they were doing press for the series finale. Jay had even come, the first and only time he made the trek to L.A with her. But at the time, she'd wished she'd been able to say goodbye to the town itself.

She hadn't fully realized how much Misty Harbor felt like home until she left.

Twelve years had changed her. She was no longer a teenager, for one thing. As she left the inn on foot and wandered down Main Street, she shouldn't have been surprised Misty Harbor had changed, too.

Sure, the differences were small, but they were altering the image she'd held for over a decade. On this fine late spring morning, a handful of kids climbed over the new play structure in the park next to the library, their minders watching from gleaming benches. A colorful banner advertising something called Harbor Fest was fastened between two light poles behind the playground.

An attractive new sign invited people into the old-fashioned library. Cami was tempted, but her agenda involved a belated breakfast. She could have taken advantage of the inn's self-proclaimed impeccable room service, but she wanted to stretch her legs. Plus, Selena had instructed her to keep her eye out for possible filming locations. She didn't exactly have any expertise in location scouting, but she'd been on enough location shoots to know what to look for.

Wasn't there a diner on the block past the library? They used to hit up the fifties-style joint after shooting wrapped for the day, since it was one of the only places in town that stayed open past nine. She and Jay and Nash and Ariel would grab a booth and order malted milkshakes and gossip as if they were real teenagers out with their friends after a football game, instead of what they really were—actors who played them on TV.

She found the diner, a block farther down than she remembered, but hesitated when a cute bakery across the street caught her eye. She should have something more to eat than a pastry, but the bakery looked as if it might have a better chance of a latte than the diner. And yes, she was Hollywood enough to admit she wanted a latte.

Cami fell in insta-love with Misty Harbor Bakeshop the moment she walked in and discovered it smelled like cardamom and coffee. She smiled brightly at the young person behind the counter. The man was wearing a full face of makeup and he looked like he'd be more at home in Echo Park than Misty Harbor—yet another sign the town had changed even more than she'd imagined.

She kept the bright smile on her face as the employee said, "Welcome to the Bakeshop, what can I get you?" Then his eyes widened. "Oh, shit. Camille Corsair. Oh, shit. Shit. I need to stop saying shit." He clamped a hand over his mouth, as if that would prevent him from saying anything more.

Cami found herself giggling. Usually being recognized when she was trying to go about her business made her feel slightly vulnerable and off-kilter, but she had to admit that dynamic was different here. The residents of Misty Harbor had put up with *Sawyer's Cove* for three years, with the occasional street closures and calls for extras, and that one time they'd set up an entire fake carnival on the beach boardwalk. But the locals never made the cast and crew feel unwelcome. She hoped the hospitality would return if what she had planned came to fruition.

"Hi," she said, scanning the retro white-on-black letter sign hanging behind the counter. "Can I get the biggest latte you have? Skim, if you have it. And, um…" She inspected the glossy pastries in the case, and her mouth instantly watered. "I don't know. What else is good?"

The employee narrowed his magenta-shadowed eyes. "What else is good? Is this a joke? Are you actually Camille Corsair, or are you just a really good cosplayer?"

*Cosplayer?* "No, I'm Camille. What's your name?"

"I'm Trevor."

"Okay. You can call me Cami."

Trevor grinned with carmine-painted lips. "Cami, oh my God. Okay. Well, *Cami*, everything in this bakeshop is going to be the best thing you ever ate, so you can't go wrong. And we're still serving breakfast for—" he consulted the big analog clock on the wall behind him "—six minutes."

Cami ordered quickly. Eggs, toast, and a side of three berry jam.

"Zelda, she's the owner, makes the jam herself. And the bread, obviously. Prepare for a taste bud explosion." Trevor keyed in the order and started making her latte.

Cami laughed again. "Where was this place when I was young enough to actually eat croissants with no consequences?"

"I know, right?" Trevor nodded as if he was intimately acquainted with actress problems. "Zelda opened it about five years ago."

She paid in cash and dropped a large denomination bill in the tip jar. It never hurt to have a friend who worked at a bakery. She was already planning the standing order they'd have to treat the crew once a week. If everything worked out. She had to remember not to get ahead of herself.

Trevor handed over her latte, and she asked, "Why did you think I was a cosplayer?"

"It's Thursday," Trevor said, as if that explained everything.

She arched an eyebrow.

Trevor waved his arms theatrically as he elaborated, "Thursdays, Fridays, and Saturdays are *Sawyer's Cove* walking tours. Sometimes the guides dress up—usually they pick iconic outfits from the show, like the homecoming dance episode, or that horrible bridesmaid dress they made you wear in the one where your long-lost half-sister got married. But sometimes the people on the tour dress up, too."

"Wait. Walking tours? I don't get it."

"It's all part of, what is it called—fan tourism. *Sawyer's Cove* has a lot of fans, and we've got an entire cottage industry here in Misty Harbor to cater to them."

"That's what I'm counting on," Cami said under her breath. Louder, she asked, "Where does the tour start? Do I need a ticket?"

"*You* want to take the *Sawyer's Cove* tour?" Trevor asked. "This day is just too weird. Jay's in here all the time, but having you come in—it's like I'm actually living in Cloudy Cove."

"Life imitating art, again, I guess." Cami shrugged, even as her heart raced at getting confirmation that Jay was indeed in Misty Harbor. She sipped her excellent latte. "Trevor, this is exactly what I needed. Thank you."

"Anytime. Wait. Seriously, what *are* you doing here?"

A slim, dark-haired woman who looked about her age came out of the back holding a paper box. Her apron was embroidered with the name "Zelda."

"Stop interrogating the customers, Trevor. Here's your breakfast, sweetie."

Cami took the box, with a grateful smile. It wasn't that she didn't want to tell Trevor what she was doing in Misty Harbor, but it was for sure against the NDA she'd signed. "Thanks. Right now I'm going to eat, but I'll be back."

"We close at six." Zelda winked. "Tell your friends."

Cami took her breakfast and headed for the beach, considering the appealing storefronts she passed with fresh eyes. As the stand-in for the fictional Cloudy Cove, Misty Harbor had performed the role perfectly. She could all too easily see the town turned into a temporary backlot once again.

She was almost at the beach when she passed a bar. The simple sign on the weathered brick exterior read "The Cove" in a typeface reminiscent of the show's. Wow. The town had really gone all in on this fan tourism thing. This place probably served theme cocktails, like Sawyer's Angst or Amy Green Apple Martinis.

She made a mental note to check out the bar later, then spotted an empty bench where she could look out over the water and eat. Her brain whirred as she processed meeting Trevor and seeing how embedded *Sawyer's Cove* already was in Misty Harbor's DNA.

She was aware that in the years since it had been unceremoniously canceled, the show's audience had actually grown. They had always seemed to generate a lot of buzz, but the audience hadn't seemed to find it until it was off the air. Cami enjoyed hearing from fans who'd come to the show late, but she'd always assumed all that was ancient history. Then other cult favorites that spoke to some nostalgic part of the culture started getting revived as limited series and garnering nice deals. And about six months ago, Selena had called to pitch her on a reboot of *Sawyer's Cove*. She wanted them to do it together; Selena would be the showrunner, and Cami would produce in addition to reprising her role as Amy Green.

*Speak of the devil,* Cami thought as her phone buzzed. She set aside her breakfast box and pulled her phone from the pocket of her skirt.

"What's up, Selena?"

"You said you'd call me when you got there," Selena said in her usual no-nonsense tone. For years, Cami had assumed Selena had no use for her, but over the past few months, she'd learned that was just how Selena was— dry as dust, with no time for preambles or bullshit of any kind. Since Cami spent her life being professionally nice, Selena's lack of pretense was refreshing, now that she was used to it anyway. Selena didn't care if Cami was sweet or friendly. She didn't believe you caught more flies with honey, not in Hollywood. She'd parlayed her *Sawyer's Cove* assistant writer gig—her very first paying job in TV—into a full-fledged staff writer job by the time the show was canceled. She'd been a staff writer ever since, but she'd never been a showrunner. That was going to change as soon as the studio put its money where its mouth was and officially green-lit the *Sawyer's Cove* reboot.

And they wouldn't do that until Cami had Jay Orlando's signature on the contract.

"I'm sorry. I was so tired last night, I passed right out, then I slept in. I'm about to eat," she added pointedly.

"Well, I'm glad you got some rest." Selena didn't sound glad, but Cami knew that didn't mean anything. "So, what's the town like? Is this going to work?"

"The town looks better than ever, and I'm getting tons of ideas based on some new stuff downtown. The people are nice. They seem to have a whole little tourism thing built up around the show."

"I told you there was an audience for this. What's the deal with Jay? You close to tracking him down?"

"Give me more than five minutes, okay? I'll find him."

Selena had been more irritated than worried when they hadn't been able to locate Jay Orlando. He didn't have an agent anymore, and he'd never had a manager. None of his old numbers worked, and Cami had felt weird about randomly calling places in Misty Harbor, looking for a lead on him. When the project she was filming in Toronto was unceremoniously cut short, she'd had the idea of simply poking around Misty Harbor until he crawled out from whatever rock he'd been hiding under.

"Okay, text me the minute he signs the contract. I have a call with Brad and Krista tomorrow, and I'd love to be able to tell them we're set. Gotta go."

Selena clicked off before Cami could say goodbye, but she didn't take it personally. She put her phone away and settled back on her bench.

Her eggs were a little cold, but still tasty. The jam was sinfully good—tart and sweet. As she ate, she glanced around the waterfront. The June sun glinted off the Atlantic. To her left was the marina, with dozens of gleaming boats lined up like oversized toys in the bath. To her right was the boardwalk, with a parking lot on one side, the rocky beach on the other. A few joggers, a group of women chatting as they pushed strollers, and a galloping golden retriever playing fetch with its owner completed the idyllic picture of coastal New England.

Cami closed her eyes against the sun, too lazy to get her sunglasses out of her bag. She imagined the rays were powering her up to face the hardest part of her mission in Misty Harbor—convincing Jay Orlando, her first boyfriend, the boy who broke her heart, to co-star with her on a reboot of the show where they'd fallen in love, both on and off screen.

She smiled wryly to herself. It sounded like the premise of a bad episode of soapy television.

# Acknowledgments

Thank you to my readers and author friends who encouraged me to write this story even though it wasn't "in my lane." I feel strongly that everyone deserves to find love and a happily ever after if that's something they're looking for in life, and Crosby is no exception.

Thanks, as ever to my writing community, especially to the KBR crew for inspiration, advice, and encouragement. Thanks to the SALT plotters for keeping my plot engines revving. Thanks to my local writer friends who make this job so much more enjoyable than if it was just me typing alone in my kitchen.

Thanks to Word Slayers and Tracy Finistrella for fantastic editing. All mistakes are mine.

If you liked this story and want more small-town m/m romance, I invite you to check out the works of Elle Waters—my not-so-secret pen name under which I write exactly that. You can check out Elle Waters books right now at https://ellewatersbooks.substack.com.

And thank you for reading!

# About the Author

Libby Waterford is the author of the Sawyer's Cove: The Reboot and the Never a Bride series. She's obsessed with her pollinator garden, DIY fermentation, and writing swoony first kisses and hopeful happily ever afters. Her steamy contemporary romances mix witty banter and all the feels with a solid dollop of good old-fashioned sexual tension. Libby wrangles her two ever-growing sons and a husband in Fairfield County, Connecticut.

Get a free story at libbywaterford.com and email Libby at libby@libbywaterford.com.

facebook.com/LibbyWaterford

instagram.com/libbywritesromance

bookbub.com/authors/libby-waterford

goodreads.com/libbywaterford

amazon.com/author/libbywaterford

www.ingramcontent.com/pod-product-compliance
Lightning Source LLC
Chambersburg PA
CBHW061534310726
48972CB00008B/2451